### "Go back to wherever you came from,"

Sara told Morgan firmly, ignoring the glint in his eye and the flutter in her chest.

"No, I don't think so." Morgan gave Sara a roguish grin as he stepped out of his wet shoes.

"You don't think what?"

"I don't think I'll be leaving."

"You can't stay here!"

"I don't see why not. You're my wife, and I'm certain that this small . . . misunderstanding can be worked out."

"Morgan, we do not have a 'small misunderstanding'! We may not be divorced, but we should be. What happened tonight was merely an irrelevant, isolated incident."

"I'm not leaving."

"This is outrageous!" Sara exclaimed. "You can't just come back and . . . move in! I'll call the authorities and have you *dragged* out!"

"Fine," he said cheerfully. He pulled the T-shirt over his head. Chest hair curled in dark whorls against his tanned skin. "They can find me in the shower."

Dear Reader,

It's March—and spring is just around the corner. We all know spring is the season of love, but at Silhouette Romance, every season is romantic, and every month we offer six heartwarming stories that capture the laughter, the tears, the sheer joy of falling in love. This month is no exception!

*Honey, I'm Home* by Rena McKay is a delightful reminder that even the most dashing hero is a little boy at heart, and Lindsay Longford's *Pete's Dragon* will reaffirm your belief in the healing power of love...and make-believe. The intense passion of Suzanne Carey's *Navajo Wedding* will keep you spellbound, the sizzling *Two To Tango* by Kristina Logan will quite simply make you want to dance, and Linda Varner's *As Sweet as Candy* will utterly charm you.

No month is complete without our special WRITTEN IN THE STARS selection. This month we have the exciting, challenging Pisces man in Anne Peters's *Storky Jones Is Back in Town*.

Throughout the year we'll be publishing stories of love by all your favorite Silhouette Romance authors—Diana Palmer, Suzanne Carey, Annette Broadrick, Brittany Young and many, many more. The Silhouette Romance authors and editors love to hear from readers, and we'd love to hear from *you!*

Happy Reading!

Valerie Susan Hayward
Senior Editor

# RENA McKAY

# Honey, I'm Home

Published by Silhouette Books New York

**America's Publisher of Contemporary Romance**

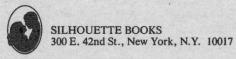

**SILHOUETTE BOOKS**
300 E. 42nd St., New York, N.Y. 10017

HONEY, I'M HOME

ISBN: 0-373-08853-1

First Silhouette Books printing March 1992

Printed in the U.S.A.

**Books by Rena McKay**

Silhouette Romance

*Bridal Trap* #36
*Desert Devil* #92
*Valley of Broken Hearts* #239
*The Singing Stone* #291
*Golden Echo* #347
*Just You and Me* #713
*Honey, I'm Home* #853

## *RENA McKAY*

currently lives in Oregon, and has long been interested in Scotland. She, her husband and mother recently traveled to Scotland to look up the castle that once belonged to some of her ancestors. In addition to traveling and castles, Rena also likes reading, cats and long walks on the beach.

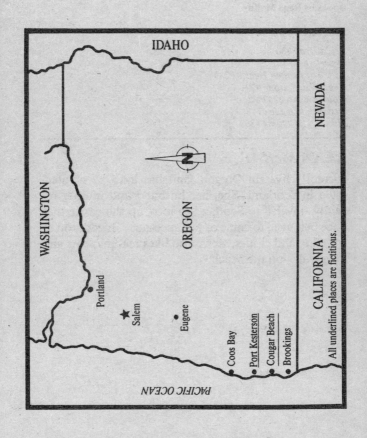

IDAHO

NEVADA

WASHINGTON

OREGON

CALIFORNIA

Portland

Salem

Eugene

Coos Bay

Port Kesterson

Cougar Beach

Brookings

PACIFIC OCEAN

All underlined places are fictitious.

# Chapter One

The first out-of-the-ordinary thing that Sara McKenzie noticed was the bottle of champagne in her refrigerator. Dom Perignon. Since when had she started stocking expensive champagne?

Then she realized Brian must have sneaked the champagne into her refrigerator as a surprise. How sweet of him . . . and how unexpectedly romantic! He must be planning a little private celebration before they announced their engagement to his parents at dinner this evening. Perhaps he also planned to surprise her with the engagement ring.

She glanced at her watch and seeing that it was already almost seven o'clock she hurried down the hall. She'd barely have time to shower and dress before Brian picked her up at seven-thirty. She always kept her secondhand store open until six-thirty on Fridays, but she'd been late closing this evening because a woman had taken her time browsing through the children's clothing. Luckily the store and apartment were attached so she didn't have to go far to change.

Just outside the bathroom she stumbled across the second out-of-the-ordinary item. A blue nylon knapsack. Definitely *not* something Brian might have dropped there. She had some used knapsacks in the store, but this one didn't look familiar. And how could it have gotten in here?

Suddenly apprehensive, she peered cautiously into the bathroom. A pile of clothing lay on the floor: faded jeans, black sweatshirt, scuffed boots. There were puddles of water and a wet towel by the shower door, and shaving gear on the bathroom counter.

A man had taken a shower in her bathroom! Some strange man had come right into her living quarters and made himself at home. And, from the looks of things, it was quite possible that he was still here!

Common sense told her the first thing she should do was to run for the phone in the kitchen and call the police. The intruder could be dangerous, perhaps even armed. She peered around, half expecting him to leap out of the hall closet. A moment later logic reminded her that was unlikely, not unless he'd managed to fold himself up small enough to fit on one of the shelves.

There was only one place he could be. The bedroom. She took a deep, steadying breath and inched silently along the hallway away from the bedroom, sliding her shaky hands along the wall for support.

A muffled noise from the bedroom stopped her. She held her breath as she listened to the sounds. Was he going through her bureau drawers, perhaps looking for cash from the store?

No, it was a different sound. She tiptoed a cautious step toward the open bedroom door. And when she did, indignation halfway overruled her fear. The man was snoring! He had come into her house, showered in her bathroom, and now he was snoring in her bed!

She reached into the bathroom and grabbed the first thing she could to use as a protective weapon. She tiptoed toward the darkened bedroom and paused just outside. She could vaguely make out a shape on the bed. Another noise made her realize that if he woke he'd instantly see her silhouetted in the open doorway. She dodged inside the room and waited with bated breath to see if she'd disturbed him.

No, he had just shifted position. He made another muffled, snorting noise. As her eyes adjusted to the dim light in the bedroom she could see dark hair against the pillow, a bare back, half a bare buttock, and long legs.

A *naked* man was snoring in her bed.

She was half-inclined to yell indignantly at him to get the hell out of there, but common sense told her that would be both foolish and dangerous. He could be some perverted weirdo. Letting her curiosity bring her into such proximity to him had been foolish enough.

Carefully she edged back toward the door. The man on the bed moved again, flinging an arm across the second pillow and bringing it closer to his body.

The movement had a peculiar familiarity. Sara took a step nearer the bed. The back also looked a little familiar, as did the legs...and when the sheet slid aside to expose a few more inches of buttock, she gasped. She'd know that lean backside anywhere!

"Morgan!" She reached for the switch by the door and flipped on the bedroom light. "Morgan, what are you doing here...what do you mean by this...Morgan, how dare you?" The words sputtered out of her in chaotic fury.

"Wh-what?" He sat up, blinking and shaking his head. His dark hair tumbled into his eyes. The sheet barely covered his pelvis, but he didn't seem concerned. Then he smiled at her, that rogue-angel smile that for so long had melted her heart and muddled her senses. "Sara. Hi. You look great."

There were about five thousand words, none of them nice, that she wanted to shout at him, and they all tried to come out at once. "You can't come in here...three years ... damn you! ... no right ... irresponsible ... my life ... Get out!"

"Now calm down," he soothed. "You're not making a single bit of sense. You'll have plenty of time to yell at me and get it all out of your system, so you don't have to say everything right now." He looked calm and relaxed and cheerful, better-looking than such an infuriating a man had a right to be.

His body was still long and lean, his chest laced with smooth muscle, his dark eyes flashing amusement at her fury. He'd acquired a tiny, crescent-shaped scar on his jaw, and a few more sun lines radiated from his eyes, but somehow the small flaws only added to an already potent physical attractiveness.

He stretched his arms overhead, and Sara suddenly realized he was about to stand up, quite unconcerned about his nudity. But *she* was very concerned about it indeed.

"Morgan, I don't know how you got in here, much less *why* you're here, but you have no right to come into my home, make a mess in my bathroom, sleep in my bed—"

"What's that you're holding?" he inquired.

"I thought you were a dangerous intruder. A burglar, a mugger, or an insane maniac. So I grabbed a weapon—"

"What were you planning to do? Curl me to death?"

She looked down at the object in her hands. A curling iron. She had been planning to defend herself with a curling iron. With as much dignity as possible she set it on her dressing table and went back to the original issue. She was not going to let him sidetrack her. He had always been much too good at that. Especially in a bedroom.

"What are you doing here?" she demanded.

"I didn't want to disturb you while you were busy in the store, so I thought I'd just take a quick nap until you closed up." Morgan spoke as if this was the most reasonable explanation in the world, when in truth it was no explanation at all for his outrageous behavior. "I was kind of beat after the long trip."

She purposely did not inquire, long trip from where? Instead she snapped, "I am not concerned about your need for a nap. I mean *why* are you here? Why, after all these years—"

"Three years can hardly be called 'all these years,'" he protested mildly. "Three years and seven months, to be exact. And you really should keep your doors more securely locked. Almost anyone could get in the back way, just as I did."

Brian had also warned her about keeping doors locked, and she tried to remember to do it, even though there was so little crime in Port Kesterson that such precautions hardly seemed necessary. Then she remembered something.

"I did lock the back door today. I specifically remember doing it because I put some milk out for a stray cat that's been hanging around."

Morgan shook his head and smiled tolerantly. "I guess that's one of the things I love about you, the way you always have a place in your heart for one more stray, homeless creature."

The implication was clear. She shelved the part of the statement about his loving her and zeroed in on the part about stray, homeless creatures. "If you have some fantastic idea that I am going to take *you* in, forget it. And you still haven't explained how you got in here."

"I guess maybe I picked the lock," he admitted. "I spent a couple of months working with a rather shady private investigator. He taught me a few things that occasionally come in useful, such as how to pick cheap locks. I also learned how to hot-wire a car."

"Terrific. Just what every responsible citizen needs to know." Morgan's résumé could list enough jobs, many of them strange and unusual, to fill an instruction pamphlet on how to mess up your life. It suddenly made her all the more appreciative of Brian's solid dependability at the bank.

"By the way, I like the name of your place," Morgan said. "Junque and Stuffe. That's very clever."

"The store was named before I got it, so compliments on my cleverness will get you nowhere," Sara said.

"But you always were great at finding bargains at garage sales and flea markets. Smart of you to turn junk and stuff into 'junque and stuffe.'"

Of course she was great at finding garage-sale bargains. Also coupon bargains, free offers and just plain doing without. It was the only way they'd managed to survive while they were married. Most of the time they had lived as if they'd taken a vow of poverty, and seeing the country while blithely trying to live on love was not all it was cracked up to be.

"I'll bet you're very good at running a secondhand store," Morgan added.

She noted that he had Junque and Stuffe pegged for what it was. Brian's parents insisted on maintaining the illusion that she owned a quaint little antique store. She did come across an occasional antique, but most of her secondhand merchandise was definitely post-antique. Not that any of this made any difference to Brian, of course. He just shrugged at his family's stuffy attitudes and occasionally enjoyed shocking them himself, such as when he bought a flashy little red Alfa Romeo convertible instead of one of the staid sedans of which they approved.

"My store is no concern of yours. I just want you to get your clothes on and get out of here. And don't forget your shaving gear in the bathroom." Then, before he threw back the sheet and exposed what little wasn't already exposed, she said briskly, "I'll be in the kitchen."

"Does that mean the condemned man gets a meal before he's thrown out in the cold, cruel world?"

"No."

"But I brought champagne," he protested.

She turned to face him again. "You? *You* put the Dom Perignon in my refrigerator? Why?"

"I thought our getting back together deserved a little something special with which to celebrate the occasion."

"Morgan, we will get back together when the *ocean* turns to champagne, when my stray cat wins the lottery, when radishes are more valuable than rubies, when—"

"Okay, I get the picture," Morgan soothed. "You're still a little upset. We'll talk about it later."

"There isn't going to be any *later*," Sara stated. "We're divorced, remember? Now get dressed and get out of here."

"Why are you so afraid of seeing me naked? In the two years and eight months of married life that we spent together, I do believe you saw me naked any number of times. Or are you afraid that seeing me in the buff might arouse irresistible memories? Such as the time we found that hidden little lake in Colorado, and we stripped off our clothes and went skinny-dipping and then—"

She stopped him before he could go into further details about what had happened then. "That was different," she said firmly. "We were married."

"It appears," Morgan said nonchalantly, "that we still are."

*"What?"*

He stood up, dragging the sheet with him and fashioning it into a makeshift sarong around his waist. His muscular chest looked darkly masculine against the sheet femininely sprigged with tiny flowers.

"Just so you won't be overcome by an uncontrollable passion at the sight of my manly charms," he explained. "You do insist that I get dressed, and I have to get my clean clothes out of my knapsack."

"Morgan, I don't give a damn about your clothes. You can dance naked up and down Highway 101 for all I care—"

"Now there's an interesting idea that hadn't occurred to me. But then, you always did have fun ideas. Like wanting to make love in that famous fountain in Rome—"

She refused to acknowledge that she'd ever had such ridiculous ideas. And they'd never reached Rome. They hadn't had the money. "I'm only interested in an explana-

tion of what you just said about our still being married. I
want to know *now*."

"It's a long story," he said. "I'll get dressed and then
we'll have a glass of champagne and talk about it." He
started down the hallway, trailing the flowered sheet and the
clean, woodsy scent of her soap.

"You're just making up this stuff about our still being
married," Sara accused. She followed him out of the bedroom door. "There isn't a word of truth in it."

Morgan stopped so short that she almost bumped into
him. "Why would I do that?" He sounded honestly surprised.

"I don't know. To drive me crazy. To ruin my plans. To
mess up my life."

"Sara, I didn't come here to hurt you or mess up your
life. I came because we made a terrible mistake three and a
half years ago, and now, through what some might call a
merry mix-up, we have a chance to correct that mistake."

He picked up the knapsack and stepped into the bathroom. When he didn't seem concerned about closing the
door while he dressed, she yanked it shut herself.

"*If* we are still married, there's definitely been a mix-up.
But I see nothing merry about it—"

"If you insist on having a closed door between us," he
chided, "you'll have to speak louder."

She raised her voice. "Morgan, I don't see how we could
possibly still be married. I received divorce papers, you
know."

"I'll be out in a minute and then we'll talk. Just don't get
all upset," he urged gently. "Everything's going to be fine.
Why don't you find some nice glasses for the champagne? I
always liked that pair we got to celebrate our first anniversary, the ones with the little stars etched on them."

"I sold them." Sara swallowed, remembering what a
painful decision that had been. Yet it had also been something she *needed* to do to put a final punctuation mark on

the end of their marriage. "I got rid of everything." Not that there had been much to get rid of.

Silence from the bathroom followed her statement, a silence that somehow sent accusing vibrations through the closed door. He had no right, she fumed, to make her feel guilty for getting rid of some foolish, sentimental mementos. Nor had he any right to work on her emotions by bringing up memories of their life together. Such as the one of that first anniversary.

They'd been broke as usual, but they'd hocked something and bought a bottle of champagne and those two glasses, and then they'd celebrated their anniversary on a moonlit Florida beach. They'd linked arms to drink the champagne, and they'd danced barefoot in the sand to the strains of music floating on the breeze from some expensive hotel nearby.

Oh, damn, damn, damn . . .

She didn't know whether she was damning him or herself, or maybe just the cruel fact that you really couldn't live on love, that eventually you had to grow up and face harsh reality.

But she didn't have time to dwell on this because a noise at the door startled her into realizing what time it was. Seven-fifteen and Brian was here, a bit early as usual. Her fiancé was at the door, and her ex-husband . . . except maybe, if what he claimed was actually true, he wasn't her *ex*-husband . . . was dressing in her bathroom. At least hopefully he *was* dressing—

Oh, Lord, now what?

She didn't want to be dishonest with Brian. It wasn't as if he didn't know she'd been married, of course. She'd told him all about it. But she'd also told him she was divorced, and introducing Brian to a man who claimed he was still her husband, before she even knew what that was all about, did not sound like the best of ideas.

She tapped on the bathroom door. "You have to get out of here. *Now.*"

"Your wish is my command, darlin', but it appears that this bathroom doesn't even have a window to crawl out of."

True enough. And the door Brian was knocking on did have a window. If she tried to sneak Morgan past that door and let him out through the store, Brian might see him.

The bathroom door opened. Morgan stood there in a clean pair of jeans only slightly less faded than the pair still on the floor. He was still barefoot and shirtless, and he looked rumpled and sexy and a little threatening.

"This is not exactly the warm welcome I had hoped for," he grumbled.

"Someone is at the door. I don't want him to see you."

"What's that supposed to mean? That you're ashamed of me?"

More knocking. "Sara?" Brian called.

"It means my fiancé is at the door, and I'd really rather not try to explain you to him at this moment."

A line crinkled Morgan's forehead beneath the tousle of dark hair. "Fiancé?" He seemed taken aback by the term.

"Morgan, I must have an explanation about this claim of yours that we're still married, but I haven't time for it now. Brian and I are expected at his parents' home in just a few minutes for a very important dinner. You'll just have to keep out of sight until we leave."

"You want me to run and hide in a closet or under the bed while you waltz off with some other guy?" Morgan asked in an incredulous tone. "No way. You're my wife and—"

He sounded as if he were ready to march out and confront Brian on the spot. She tried the only weapon she had left. "Morgan, if there was any truth in your statement that you didn't come here to hurt me or mess up my life, you won't stand there and argue. You'll just hide now and we can get this straightened out later."

More noise from the door. "Sara, are you all right?"

"Impatient little devil, isn't he?" Morgan grumbled. He hesitated, but finally he said, "Okay, just for you I'll do it. Just for you I'll run and hide like some guilty lover dodging a returning husband. But just don't forget,'' he added warningly, *''I'm* the husband here.''

*We'll see about that,* Sara thought, but she didn't say anything. She was running out of time. She reached into the bathroom and grabbed Morgan's arm. She led him to the bedroom and shoved him inside. ''You don't have to hide under the bed or in the closet. Just keep the door closed and don't come out. Take another nap or something.'' Then another dismaying thought struck her. ''Is your car parked where Brian can see it?''

''I didn't come by car. I came on a bicycle. It's in the parking area beside the store.''

A bicycle. Morgan McKenzie had ridden back into her life on a bicycle. It figured.

Sara closed the bedroom door, caught sight of the incriminating pile of clothes on the bathroom floor and hurriedly stuffed them in the clothes hamper. Finally she got to the kitchen, where Brian was peering through the glass portion of the door. When Sara unlocked the door, which Morgan had apparently relocked after his break-in, Brian's surprised stare quickly turned to a frown.

''You're not dressed.'' Brian was wearing a dark suit and silk tie that emphasized his blond good looks. Dinners at the Athertons, unless the occasion was specified as a barbecue, were never casual. They considered themselves the First Family of Port Kesterson and dressed and entertained in a manner befitting that lofty position.

''I know. I'm sorry. I had to keep the store open late, and then I lay down to nap for just a minute and I guess I overslept.'' She managed a yawn, the size of which she hoped concealed a certain lack of authenticity. With Morgan hiding in her bedroom, she felt anything but relaxed and yawny.

''Sara, I don't know why you feel you have to keep the store open such long hours, or why you let people just keep on browsing at closing time. You know how my parents feel about tardiness—''

Yes, she knew. With the Athertons, tardiness rated right up there with the awful sins of having a fondness for country and western music or wearing polyester plaid.

"You're early. We still have plenty of time," Sara said soothingly. "Just sit down and watch TV for a minute. We can drink the champagne—"

She broke off. She'd originally had it in her head that Brian had brought the champagne for a little celebration, and the thought had apparently stuck in spite of facts later revealed to the contrary.

"Champagne?" Brian repeated.

"Nothing. Never mind. I'll just be a few minutes."

Her shower would have impressed the most conscientious water-saving environmentalist, and she brushed her teeth with a speed that would have appalled her dentist. Darn, she should have retrieved her clothes out of the bedroom before she'd showered—

She reached for the robe that usually hung on the back of the bathroom door. No robe. She had put it in the load of washing she'd done that morning, and it must still be in the dryer.

The jeans and blouse she'd taken off were in a wet pile on the floor, courtesy of the leaky shower curtain.

That left just one item to cover her when she went to the bedroom to get her clothes for the evening. The towel.

She hesitated uneasily. Wearing only a towel while dashing into a darkened bedroom where Morgan was hiding did not strike her as the wisest or safest of actions. She remembered how he used to pat dusting powder lovingly all over her body after they'd showered together.

Then she scoffed at her fears. Morgan, who had peacefully fallen asleep under the stars the night their motorcycle had broken down about a hundred miles from nowhere in New Mexico, was probably already asleep again by now. He had never been one to lie awake fussing and worrying.

She secured the towel firmly around her body and tiptoed down the hallway. She could hear faint sounds from the

TV in the living room as Brian impatiently flipped channels. With the stealth of a cat burglar she eased the bedroom door open. It closed behind her without any help from her.

The heavy drapes were drawn, and without the open door to shed some light into the dark bedroom she couldn't see a thing. But she could feel. A feathery stroke across her back, the imprint of lips on her shoulder.

"Morgan, don't do that!" she whispered fiercely.

No words from Morgan, not even the sound of his breathing. But the feathery touches on her body continued, fingertip whispers over her shoulders, across the exposed slope of one breast, into the valley, over the other breast. She stood as if her feet had been welded to the carpet, momentarily unable to move. Strange waves of heat washed over her in dizzying succession. She swayed, oddly disoriented, and he caught her.

The touch of strong, solid fingers on her arms broke the momentary spell. She turned around, put her hands against his bare chest and pushed.

"I came to get my clothes. Please take your hands off me."

If she thought the request, phrased with frigid politeness, would have any effect on him, she was wrong.

He brushed her hands aside and pulled her closer. The heat of his bare chest penetrated the towel. One arm clamped around her waist while the other hand roamed with a pirate's audacity over her curves. She braced her feet and pulled back, but the action only arched her body closer against his pelvis. And loosened the tight wrap of the towel.

"Morgan, stop that." There was more panic than ice in her voice now. She edged an arm between them to hold the towel in place. "I'm warning you, I'll scream—"

"Will you?" he challenged. She could hear the laughter in his voice. "Okay, scream."

His lips whispered over her face, her eyes, her lips, her throat. This is outrageous, she fumed to herself. His hand

slid to the bottom hem of the towel, and a fingertip traced
its edge across her thigh. I will scream, I really will, she told
herself.

Then Brian would come running, and here she'd be, having to admit that this man holding her wasn't exactly a
stranger, that she'd come into the room wearing nothing but
a towel even though she knew he was here. She'd have to
explain that she had, in fact, *asked* him to hide in her bedroom, and why.

And while her mind was racing as fast...and as use-
lessly...as a spinning top, his mouth ravished her with
kisses. Butterfly kisses, rainbow kisses, kisses of velvet and
fire.

"Sara, kiss me," he whispered. "I've been waiting more
than three and a half years for you to kiss me."

"No..."

One arm still held her around the waist, but the other
hand lifted to caress the underside of her chin. Slowly,
seemingly against her will, because her conscious mind kept
furiously insisting *I will not kiss you!* her face lifted to his.

He groaned softly as his mouth covered hers. Over three
years, she thought wildly, over three years...

Her inner dialogue with herself changed to cover the situation. She may have lost one small battle of wills, but this
would go no further. She would not kiss him back nor let
him kiss her the way they used to kiss before they made
love...while they were making love...

His tongue teased the line of her clamped lips, and the tiniest of partings, no more than a sliver of remembered desire, separated the tightly pressed muscles. *No,* she vowed,
*I will not let you in.*

The tip of his tongue crept into the opening, and still she
was saying *no.* And then he was kissing her the way he had
so many times before, making her feel the way no other man
ever had. Making her head spin and her skin tingle and her
toes lift to bring her closer to him.

His hand crept to the towel, but some remnant of control made her grab the towel and hold it tight before it could slip away and leave nothing but tempting memories between her breasts and his chest. He rubbed lightly against her, caressing her with his body, and she fought against an awakening core of yearning. His teeth fastened to her earlobe with gentle fierceness, the imprint stirring slumbering nerves deep inside her. Her skin felt exquisitely, sharply sensitive beneath the caress of his lips.

"Sara? You about ready?" Brian called.

Morgan laughed softly, hinting at a wickedly intimate interpretation of Brian's innocent words. Sara fumbled frantically for the light switch.

That perhaps wasn't the greatest idea, either. She should simply have grabbed the first thing she could reach in her closet and run. But it was too late now. The light was on, and she was standing there wearing nothing but a skimpy towel and a rosy glow of embarrassment and anger.

Morgan whistled softly as he looked her up and down. "You've gained a few pounds," he said. "And in all the right places."

"I have not!" she said hotly, then amended grudgingly, "Well, maybe one or two."

A bold fingertip reached to caress one of those "right" places, but she dodged it and held the towel so tightly around her that she could hardly breathe. She berated herself for getting drawn into this ridiculous discussion about her body. She surreptitiously gave the towel a little yank to make certain not so much as a smidgen of breast curve was exposed.

But Morgan just grinned and ran a finger along the bottom edge of the towel, emphasizing the fact that her upward twist on the towel had only left other areas far less than adequately concealed.

"Thank heaven for skimpy towels," he murmured appreciatively.

Sara decided to ignore the shortcomings of the towel and concentrate on just getting out of the bedroom as quickly as possible. She marched to the closet. Morgan followed her and peered at the contents with her.

"What sort of evening is this?" he asked.

"That's none of your business."

"Something special with his parents, I believe you said. Hmm. Offhand, I'd guess they're rich, probably conservative and stuffy. I'd suggest that blue, silky-looking thing. They'll approve of both the color and the discreet neckline." He pulled the cowl-necked dress on its padded hanger out of the closet. "The red would look gorgeous with your dark hair and vivid coloring, and your body really deserves that plunging neckline, but I suspect that would be a bit too flashy for them."

The fact that he'd pigeonholed the Athertons so accurately without ever having met either them or Brian further annoyed Sara. She'd already been planning to wear the blue, and she snatched it out of his hands.

Reluctantly she asked, "What makes you think they're rich?"

He shrugged. "As I recall, lack of money was one of our more nagging problems. It seems likely that the next time around you'd take a closer look at the prospective bridegroom's financial balance sheet. Not that it matters anyway, since you're still *my* wife." Briskly he started opening drawers. "Now, about underthings—"

She snatched things out of a drawer without even looking at them. She remembered that he'd always liked to pick out lacy lingerie for her . . . and sometimes demanded a private modeling of everything. She forced herself to suppress the memory.

"My underthings are none of your business," she stated firmly. She clutched everything and headed for the door.

He grabbed her arm and swung her around to face him. "I'm letting you go for now," he said softly. "But I'll be here when you get back. In the meantime, you can be thinking about what just happened." He brushed his thumb across her lips in intimate reminder.

She refused to acknowledge that anything had happened or that the touch on her lips sent a smoky tendril curling wickedly through her body. "I'd much rather you'd go and come back tomorrow or some other time when we can more conveniently discuss this—"

"I'll be here when you get back," he repeated. His voice had a meaningful inflection that disturbed her.

She swallowed. "All that's going to happen is that we'll *talk*—"

His fingertip touched the hollow of her throat and then drew a line into the valley between her breasts. "Is it?" he asked.

"Yes!"

Then another thought apparently occurred to him. His grip on her arm tightened. "You *are* coming home tonight, of course. You're not planning to spend the night with this guy."

"That's also none of your business!"

"Eleven o'clock," he said abruptly. "That's plenty of time for dinner and polite small talk afterward. You'll be back by eleven—or I'll come looking for you."

## Chapter Two

"Sara, it's seven-twenty-nine!"

Knowing the exact time at any given moment sometimes seemed to Sara a not too wholly appealing quality in a man, but it no doubt served Brian well in his responsible position at the bank. She was also, of course, much more time-conscious than she had been back in those carefree days with Morgan. She doubted if Morgan was any more concerned about punctuality than he had ever been...although he had sounded rather positive about eleven o'clock.

And what insufferable arrogance, trying to set a curfew as if she were some teenager on a first date!

"I'm coming," she called to Brian from the bathroom.

She shimmied into the blue dress, swept her long brunet hair into the sleek updo that she knew met Mrs. Atherton's approval and locked it in place with mousse and a massive dose of hairspray. She did a fast job on her makeup and dabbed on the perfume Brian had given her for her birthday. She should have a jacket—evenings on the Oregon coast were cool, even in the summer—but she didn't want to go back in the bedroom to get one.

Brian was standing by the door looking at his watch again, or still, when Sara finally dashed out to the kitchen.

"Sorry," she apologized once more.

He smiled and took her hands in his, the admiring head-to-toe inspection he gave her saying her appearance made up for her tardiness.

"You do look lovely. Sorry I was so impatient." He kissed her lightly on the cheek so as not to muss her lipstick. He looked terrific, too. The expensive dark suit had definitely not come from Port Kesterson's lone clothing store. "Did I hear voices? It almost sounded as if you were talking to someone in the bedroom."

"No, I was just . . . singing." She smiled gaily and tucked her hand under his elbow. "Singing with happiness about tonight."

But she was not exactly singing with happiness as they drove toward the Atherton residence situated on a wooded bluff overlooking the ocean. The road was even named for them, Atherton Drive.

She had expected to feel nervous, of course, on the occasion of this announcement. She knew that the divorced owner of a secondhand establishment called Junque and Stuffe was not the Atherton's first choice in a wife for their only son. Brian's parents undoubtedly would have preferred someone who had attended his Eastern college and who came with a suitable pedigree. She'd thought, however, that given time she could win them over.

But that was before she had an ex-husband who claimed not to be ex stashed in her bedroom . . .

Sara didn't see how Morgan's claim that they were still married could possibly be true, but she also couldn't believe that he was outright lying. Morgan had any number of character flaws: a cavalier attitude toward money, a lack of persistence, irresponsibility, procrastination, unpunctuality . . . Okay, she said to herself, you've made your point.

Morgan McKenzie is not your steadfast, Rock-of-Gibraltar type. But he had never been a liar. So the unhappy possibility existed that there could be something to what he claimed.

"You seem rather quiet tonight," Brian observed as he turned into the circular driveway of his parents' home.

"Just thinking."

"When do you think we should tell my parents our good news? Before dinner, during, after?"

Sara shivered slightly. She needed the jacket she hadn't brought. Although she wasn't certain it was the coolness of the evening that made her shiver. She suspected the Athertons were not going to look on this announcement as such "good news." Especially if they knew *all* the news.

Brian put his arms around her after he turned off the engine. Soft light from the coach lanterns beside the carved double doors of the big house dimly lit the interior of the car. "You don't need to be nervous. It isn't as if this is going to come as a big surprise to them. I think they're expecting us to tell them tonight, in fact."

"Maybe . . . maybe we should put the announcement off for a while."

"Why would we want to do that?"

Sara searched for some logical reason other than the real one, which was that she felt a certain squeamishness about announcing an engagement while the possibility existed that she was still married to another man. Doing so would surely be, at the very least, in bad taste. Worse, it struck her as thoroughly unethical.

Not immediately informing Brian of the situation with Morgan wasn't quite ethical, either. Nor were the white lies she'd told him about napping and singing. And hiding a man in her bedroom definitely held some ominous implications about her ethics.

Damn you, Morgan, she thought, suddenly furious with him again. You had no right to do any of this to me. Why didn't you just stay back there in the past where you belong?

Suddenly Sara thought of something. Earlier she'd thought Brian was going to surprise her with a ring tonight, but apparently that was not true or he'd have done it by now. Maybe it was a way to buy a little time until this mess could be straightened out.

"Perhaps it would be better if we put off telling your parents until we have a ring." Then, because she was afraid that had an unintended gimme-a-diamond sound, she added awkwardly, "I just meant that the announcement might have a more... official flavor then."

"I intended to pick one out when I was in Portland earlier this week, but a potential client wanted to play a few rounds of golf so I didn't have time. He's considering building a small shopping center here. It could be a big leap forward for Port Kesterson."

"Yes, I'm sure that was more important," Sara murmured.

On a scale of cold logic, she could see that golfing with the potential client probably was more important. Yet the fact that Brian was so willing to put bank business ahead of their engagement ring mildly dismayed her. She and Morgan had spent two days looking for just-right matching wedding bands, circles of gold with starbursts of minuscule diamonds, and then exchanged the rings in a sweet, tacky Reno wedding ceremony...

A two-day expedition that had certainly been a waste of time and effort, she reminded herself briskly, considering that the marriage had fallen considerably short of till-death-do-us-part. Yes, Brian's attitude was the right one, she assured herself. It was important to keep priorities straight. A client who wanted to build a shopping center didn't come along every day, and they could get a ring any time.

"But I don't think we should wait for the ring to tell them," Brian said. She started to make some further protest, but he squeezed her hand. "Be brave. They won't bite. And if they do, I'll protect you."

The foyer opened onto an enormous room overlooking the sea. Glass swept from corner to corner and floor to cathedral ceiling on the ocean side of the room; the focal point of the opposite wall was a huge rock fireplace. In between were conversational groupings of sofas and loveseats and chairs on a luxurious off-white carpet. At least fifteen or twenty people were in the room, which rather surprised Sara. She had thought this was to be an intimate dinner for the Athertons, Brian and herself.

She clutched Brian's hand. "I really don't think this is a good time—"

Mrs. Atherton kissed the air in the neighborhood of Sara's cheek. She repeated her son's words. "Sara, you look lovely."

"Thank you. I'm sorry we're a little late." Sara decided to skip an explanation rather than tell any more fibs.

Sara saw no one she recognized among the middle-aged and older guests. The Athertons didn't socialize much with the permanent residents of Port Kesterson. Most of their guests came from out of town or out of state, often people they'd known when they lived back East, although occasionally they entertained people from some of the expensive vacation homes in the area.

First sight of all the unfamiliar people upset Sara, but on second thought relief replaced the distress she'd felt. She and Brian obviously couldn't spring an engagement announcement on a group of strangers. The tight bands around her chest relaxed a few degrees and she took some deep breaths.

"There are so many people here I want you two to meet." Mrs. Atherton tucked her hand under her son's elbow with a light but determined possessiveness.

Mrs. Atherton was small, silver-haired and elegant. With the addition of a dapper mustache, the same description fitted Mr. Atherton, who was weaving through the guests toward them. The Athertons were in their sixties, Brian not having come along until his parents were in their forties.

Brian resisted his mother's tug. He frowned. "Mother, I thought this was going to be a small, private dinner. You know I mentioned that we had something to tell you."

Mrs. Atherton smiled brightly. "We had a few house-guests, and I couldn't just ignore them, of course, and then this lovely couple from California is buying that new place up the road—"

Brian suspected, Sara realized, that his mother had deliberately invited all these guests to forestall an announcement she did not want to hear. Sara couldn't help feeling hurt by Mrs. Atherton's maneuverings, but, given the situation with Morgan, relief still outweighed the hurt.

Suddenly Brian's jaw squared with determination. "Mother, Sara and I really must talk to the two of you."

Sara shook her head. "Brian, no, I don't think…this isn't the right time…"

Sara's protests went unheeded as Brian herded her and his parents into the side room that Mr. Atherton used as a home office. Brian held her arm just above the elbow, reassuringly pressing it close to his side. He thought, of course, that she was simply nervous about his parents' reaction to the news. He had no idea that her reluctance had to do with her suddenly ambiguous marital status. She tried again.

"Please, Brian, I really think we should wait—"

Brian put an arm around her shoulders. "Mother, Dad, Sara and I want to tell you that we are engaged to be married. We haven't set a wedding date yet, but we'd like it to be as soon as possible."

The Athertons didn't come out with direct criticism of Sara, but Mr. Atherton's eyes got that squinty look that everyone at the bank knew meant he was about to reject a loan application. He fingered his silver mustache and said, "We can't spare you at the bank for some extended honeymoon, you know."

"You've been seeing each other such a brief length of time," Mrs. Atherton said. Delicately she added, "Perhaps

you haven't had time to consider all the differences in...
backgrounds and family. And interests."

A subtle reference to Junque and Stuffe, Sara realized.
But Brian rose to the occasion.

"We've considered everything, and we *are* engaged." He
said it with a take-it-or-leave-it stubbornness. "I'll have the
ring next week."

Sara could hardly jump in and deny the announcement,
and despite her dismay, she was proud of Brian's stubborn
determination not to be sidetracked by his parents' manip-
ulations. He really was a dynamic and ambitious man, dependable and protective, and his firmness in this awkward
situation was more proof of his love for her.

The Athertons capitulated graciously. There were hugs
and kisses and a manly handshake between father and son.
Sara wasn't certain how people of the Atherton's social
standing handled engagements, but she was surprised when
they said they'd immediately announce it to their guests. She
suspected they felt that, like a root canal on a bad tooth,
they may as well get it over with.

But she could win them over, she vowed. She would.
She'd make up for all her shortcomings by dazzling them as
the world's most perfect daughter-in-law. She envisioned a
new sign at the store, something quietly elegant: Atherton's
Antiques.

Brian squeezed her arm. "See?" he whispered. "That
wasn't so bad, was it?"

Sara nodded, but what she saw in her mind was Morgan
telling her she was still married to him. Morgan sleeping in
her bed, half a buttock blithely exposed. Morgan looking at
her with dancing, smoldering eyes. Morgan kissing her,
making her feel ... not the way she wanted to feel.

Morgan could ruin everything.

Mrs. Atherton made the engagement announcement,
gaily referring to it as a delightful surprise, and identifying
Sara as the owner of a "lovely little antique store." Dinner
was late because people clustered around offering good

wishes and congratulations. Sara heard murmurs about what a striking couple she and Brian made. Then dinner dragged on interminably. Sara pushed food around on her plate and managed to make an occasional appropriate comment even though her mind kept straying to the past where this peculiar complication had begun.

Sara and Morgan had met the summer after her second year of college. He had just a few credits short of getting his degree at the University of Southern California, planning to go back and finish up in the fall. They were both working near the beach, he at a surfing shop, she at a taco stand.

It was an idyllic summer of laughing and surfing, beach parties and falling in love. In the fall he decided there really was no point in his going back to college. He was going to be a writer, and real life was a better teacher than dull college professors. Sara hadn't found her college professors dull, but her education had no particular goal and she felt no compulsion to continue it. *Living* life had indeed sounded more exciting.

In addition, there was the fact that her parents' marriage of twenty-two years had just broken up. At twenty, Sara certainly considered herself independent and adult, and yet with her parents' breakup she had the odd, lost feeling of having been set adrift. Her father was involved with a much younger woman. Her mother threw herself into a frantic round of singles' activities. Morgan and their love for each other were suddenly the only stable things in her life.

When he said *let's get married and see the world together,* she said *yes!*

They hadn't quite seen the world together, because of their persistent shortage of money, but they'd seen a good portion of the States, Canada and Mexico. They worked at whatever jobs they could find as they bounced from city to city, state to state. Morgan skipped from job to job, saying he needed as wide a range of experiences as possible as a basis for his writing career. Sara willingly followed wherever he wanted to go, sometimes even making suggestions about new places to see.

The only problem was, he never wrote anything. He kept talking about all the marvelous background and story material he was collecting, but the only writing income he ever earned was five dollars from some newspaper for a poem he'd written about littering. It had a nice social message, and he even got a fan letter from a sweet little lady who sent him directions for recycling old metal cans into wind chimes, but it didn't exactly put him on the bestseller lists.

Nor was his brief excursion into the wind chime business a roaring success. At one time he had about fifty of them hanging outside the tiny trailer they were renting. They made so much noise that one night Sara had a dream that Earth was being attacked by tiny aliens who'd arrived in cans from outer space.

Eventually she realized that all his talk of writing was just a fancy excuse for quitting jobs when he tired of them, for being irresponsible about money, for not wanting to put down roots anywhere.

As this evening at the Athertons' progressed, Sara began to hear something even more ominous than fifty clattering wind chimes: the echo of Morgan's warning about eleven o'clock. The sound got louder and louder, like the spooky music in a horror movie.

Of course Morgan wouldn't really come looking for her and make some ghastly scene, complete with announcement that she was *his* wife. Would he?

Of course not. Not that she wouldn't put it past him, but he had no idea where she was. Port Kesterson was small, but not small enough that he could storm every house looking for her.

She tried to remember if she'd given him any clues. Had she mentioned Brian's name? No, she was certain, almost certain anyway, that she had referred to Brian only as her fiancé and that no reference had been made to his name or position at the bank.

But Morgan had an unsettling talent for ferreting out facts and getting people to talk. On their wanderings around the country he was always meeting people who told him about their work and private lives, everyone from the man who told him the frightening story of a near-fatal boat trip fleeing from Cuba, to the sweet-looking elderly woman who cheerfully related risqué tales of her eight marriages.

She reassured herself with the thought that there was, however, no one for him to talk to in the bedroom.

That calmed her for all of five seconds, until it occurred to her that he wasn't exactly locked in the bedroom. It would be just like Morgan to wander into the yard and strike up a conversation with gossipy old Mrs. Denver, who tended to hang her washing on the line at odd hours of the night. It wouldn't take Morgan two minutes to find out from Mrs. Denver who Sara's fiancé was and where his parents lived.

Perhaps, she thought reluctantly, it would be wise to let Morgan win this round and simply be home by eleven o'clock. They could get this mistake or whatever it was straightened out, and she could send him on his way.

Getting home by eleven o'clock was not going to be easy, however. After dinner Brian and one of the male guests settled deep into a private conversation near the fireplace. Several times Sara nervously drifted by and tried to catch Brian's attention. She heard what she privately thought of as bank words, "development," "necessary land acquisition," "liquidity" and "FDIC regulations."

Louder than the words was the *tromp-tromp-tromp* of minutes passing, the sound of eleven o'clock approaching. She kept glancing toward the door, half expecting to see a bare-chested Morgan burst in.

By the time Brian finally came over to where a steely-eyed, beige-haired woman was quizzing Sara about her educational background, she was almost ready to kick him in the shins. You'd think on the occasion of their engagement announcement that he could forgo business talk for an evening. Her hair, fortified with enough spray to withstand hurricane and avalanche, felt as if it had a lethal strangle-hold on her head. Her stomach rumbled around indigesti-ble lumps of nervousness.

"Madeline, you're monopolizing my fiancée," Brian chided the woman with mock ferociousness, "and I'm go-ing to steal her away. Madeline was Mother's roommate at Radcliffe," he added by way of explanation to Sara.

Sara managed to smile at Madeline, who obviously was not overly impressed with Sara's two years at a California junior college.

Brian smoothly guided her out of range of the woman's interrogation. She was grateful for the rescue, but a mo-ment later she realized it was one of those frying-pan-into-fire leaps.

"I see you looking at your watch about every ten sec-onds," Brian whispered.

She momentarily thought he was scolding her for some social gaffe, and a bit cooly she said, "It is getting late—"

"And you're practically announcing to everyone that we have a more intimate celebration planned for later," Brian teased with a brush of lips against her ear. "One that you're very eager to get to."

Oh, Lord. Brian expected that now, because they were engaged, there would be a big leap in the level of intimacy in their relationship.

Frantically she searched for an emergency exit from this corner. It wasn't an unexpected corner, of course. Brian had been more patient and understanding than most men would have been with her reluctance to rush into an intimate rela-tionship, but it was hardly a surprise that he'd expect the situation to change with the announcement of their en-gagement.

But with Morgan back muddling up her life, counting off the seconds in her bedroom—

Not that Morgan was actually *in* her life, she assured herself. Not that Morgan or his kisses meant anything to her. Not that she cared what he thought about her relationship with Brian, and not that she would ever, *ever* get involved with Morgan again, but...

Oh, damn. The thoughts whirled around in her head as if she'd taken too many spins on some wild carnival ride. But of one thing she was certain. She did not want to spend tonight with Brian.

"I'd really just like to go home. I—I'm not feeling very well." No fibs there. At the moment her stomach felt as if it was on a little loop-the-loop carnival ride of its own. "I'm really sorry."

"Of course, hon." He sounded disappointed but not angry. "The Bearnaise did taste a bit off tonight. And a few minutes with Madeline is enough to upset anyone's stomach."

They made polite goodbyes to the guests, whom Sara suspected were thinking exactly what Brian had suggested, although they were too well-bred to actually snicker or leer. Sara and Brian exchanged more hugs with the Athertons and finally escaped. She leaned back in the bucket seat of Brian's car and closed her eyes.

"Perhaps a drive along the ocean and some fresh air would make you feel better," Brian suggested.

Sara's watch had shown fourteen minutes to eleven when they were in the foyer. It took exactly thirteen minutes to drive from the Atherton's to her place.

"Not tonight," she murmured.

It wasn't until Brian stopped the car in the little graveled parking area beside Junque and Stuffe that nervousness about the time stopped churning in Sara's stomach. It wasn't because she'd come in under the deadline.

It was the sight of the bicycle neatly chained to the corner post at the rear of the lot. Morgan's bicycle. All evening she had been practically rigid with the fearful vision of a wrathful Morgan rushing around town searching for her, perhaps even storming into the Athertons and dragging her off like some caveman. The idea that he'd have had to do it on a *bicycle* suddenly made her giggle.

"Sara? Are you all right?"

She managed to turn the giggle into a cough. "I'll be fine."

"I could come in and fix you a cup of tea or something—"

"No, thanks anyway. It's been a wonderful evening. Perhaps just a little too much excitement."

"I'll have the ring by next weekend."

"No rush."

He walked her to the door. The outside light was on, courtesy of Morgan. Sara hoped Brian wouldn't remember that it hadn't been on when they'd left earlier. He said he'd call or come by the following morning to see how she was. He kissed her lightly and then tested the door after she'd closed it behind her to make certain it was locked. His concern for her safety and welfare made her feel secure and protected.

She turned on the kitchen light, and the feeling of security vanished.

Morgan was leaning against the wall in the darkened hallway, arms folded. He had on jeans and a shirt, but he was barefoot and the shirt hung open and unbuttoned. He looked at his watch.

"You made it. Just barely."

"The fact that I am home at this time has nothing to do with your ridiculous deadline."

She thought about pointing out to him that if he'd huffed and puffed his bicycle up to the Athertons' place, he'd have been too winded to drag her out, but she decided to leave that alone. Seeing him standing there in the shadows, looking big and lean and darkly dangerous, she wasn't convinced he wouldn't have come after her, bicycle or no.

She set her purse on the table. "Very well," she said briskly, "let's get down to business. What is all this nonsense about our still being married?"

"Are you sure you feel like discussing this now? Your banker friend sounded very solicitous about your health when he told you good-night at the door. I hope you're not unwell." Morgan also managed to sound solicitous, but his rascal grin said he knew she'd been faking it.

Sara was not about to admit that she had used a version of the infamous I-have-a-headache-tonight-dear line on Brian. She also noted that Morgan referred to Brian as her "banker friend."

She sighed with a certain resignation. "I take it you've been snooping?"

She glanced toward the small room she used as an office. One door of the office opened onto the kitchen, the other led into the store. She could see a corner of her desk cluttered with papers.

"You're implying I went through your personal papers? Never," he declared indignantly. "What do you think I am?"

The opening was tempting, but Sara decided not to take advantage of it. Instead she said, "So how do you know Brian is a banker?"

"I spent some time down at the dock while the fishing boats were coming in. I had a cup of coffee at a little restaurant down the street. I bought a copy of the local weekly newspaper. I helped your very nice neighbor on the other side of the fence hang up her washing."

Given all that, Sara thought sourly, he probably knew everything from how long she and Brian had been seeing each other to the fact that her dentist had just commended her for having no cavities. "So what did you find out?" she asked with a certain resignation.

"I learned that everyone knows exactly who the attractive young woman is who runs Junque and Stuffe. Also that the man in your life is Brian Atherton, and he'll be running the bank as soon as his father retires. The elder Mr. Atherton isn't merely a bank employee, however. He's a major stockholder, and his son has a piece of the action, as well. The bank, and the Athertons, are very prosperous, although this may be due partly to the fact that it's the only

bank in town. The Athertons are not the most beloved of
area residents. In general, they are considered snobbish,
aloof, penny-pinching, cold, rigid, condescending, patron-
izing—''

''I can only assume you've supplied some of those words
yourself, because they don't sound like something you
picked up from the fishermen down at the dock.''

He smiled. ''Perhaps I condensed and rephrased some of
the items I heard. And cleaned up the language a bit.''

''What you've heard is quite irrelevant. It's just that
people don't really know the Athertons. Simply because
they have money and know how to handle it doesn't make
them . . .'' She floundered for a word, and finally said a bit
defensively, ''doesn't make them not nice.''

''The only thing I can't figure out is why they live here at
all, because they obviously consider themselves much too
good for the town, and Port Kesterson is not exactly a center of either social or financial activity.''

''Mrs. Atherton has a rather complex set of allergies that
unfortunately worsened as she grew older. Environmental
pollution and even the ordinary exhausts and fumes of any
large city have a very deleterious effect on her.'' Leave it to
Mrs. A. to have some sort of elite allergy profile, of course.
No common, garden-variety hay fever for her. ''They came
here because the air coming off a few thousand miles of
open ocean usually keeps her free of problems.''

''I'm sorry to hear about her health problems. But that is
no excuse for their acting like royalty among the local peas-
ants, even if they do have a road named after them. Oh,
general opinion, by the way, is that your Brian falls into the
same royal category. Sometimes a royal *pain* category. Although it is reluctantly conceded that he's the best catch in
town, and you've got him. He has the money, the car, the
secure future at the bank and the penthouse unit in the only
condo building in town. A building that was originally an
Atherton development, I understand.''

"Morgan, how could you do this? How could you wander all over town, snooping and prying and listening to ridiculous gossip—"

"Oh, you're going to make coffee. Great!"

Sara looked down to see that she was, indeed, making coffee. She'd done it automatically, without ever thinking about it. The last thing she intended to do was to play the polite hostess with Morgan, but dumping the coffee out seemed a bit childish, so she just turned her back on the coffeemaker and folded her arms.

"All of this is irrelevant, as I'm sure you realize, and you're wasting time for both of us. Let's get down to the bottom line. I've asked you about ten times now to explain your claim that we're still married, and you keep dodging the issue."

"Very well. I was, naturally, rather upset when you walked out on me—"

"I was also rather upset, or I wouldn't have walked out," Sara pointed out. She lifted her chin. "Not without good reason, I might add."

They had been right here in Oregon at the time, living in a houseboat tied at a small dock on the river near Portland. Living in a houseboat had sounded wildly romantic when a man Morgan met said they could live there free while he worked in Alaska for a few months. She had envisioned cozy elegance on the water. What they got was a shack supported by planks lashed to some old oil drums. It leaked water from both above and below and smelled like something that had been too long underwater. Once Sara and Morgan walked into a store, and another customer asked the clerk, "What *is* that odd fishy smell?"

What finished Sara was a howling storm that tore the so-called houseboat loose from its moorings. They found themselves adrift on the river, headed for the ocean, tossed by waves, sloshing in water to their knees.

Sara remembered shouting as they frantically bailed water, "If we get out of this alive, I am leaving! I have had it with living like this, pretending other people are foolish for wanting to own a nice home and have some money in the bank and be safe and secure and able to pay their bills. I am tired of being wet, dirty and broke!'' Maybe she hadn't said it all in such complete sentences, given the fact that she was cold, shaking and scared, but that was the gist of it.

For a while it looked as if they really might not get out alive, but a larger vessel came along and rescued them. By the time the boat towed them back to Portland, Sara had calmed down. A newspaper reporter was there to interview them, and it all began to seem like a memorable adventure.

Then harsh reality struck again when they had no money to rent a different place to live, not even enough money to go to a motel to dry out for a few days. Morgan had a week's wages due from a job as a chimney sweeper's assistant, but that did not impress motel clerks.

''He says the same as the others,'' Morgan reported after trying yet another motel. ''No credit card, no credit.''

Sara and Morgan had always had a certain blithe disregard, perhaps even a bit of scorn for such mundane trappings of normal life as credit cards. They were carefree playmates, and the world was their sandbox. But Sara suddenly got a totally different perspective on their situation.

She saw then that they had been flitting through life under the romantic pretense that they were footloose and carefree, unshackled by the ties that bound less free spirits to dull jobs and mortgages and crabgrass. But in truth they were nothing but penniless bums. As irrefutable proof, they didn't even possess that classic plastic symbol of American life, the credit card. Furthermore, given their irregular income and lack of permanent address, there was no way they could get one.

And suddenly Sara *wanted* a credit card; she wanted to feel the cool, smooth plastic in her hand and see her name imprinted in gold letters. She wanted to be able to walk into a store and toss down the card if she saw something she liked. She wanted a telephone number and the address of a real home, a bank account and health insurance and a car that could qualify as something other than a demolition derby contender.

They got into an incredible fight over it. Morgan, refusing to see the larger issue, said she couldn't break up a marriage over something as insignificant as a credit card. Sara defiantly said she certainly could.

Sara telephoned her mother, collect, of course, and asked for enough money to buy a ticket to San Diego. When the money arrived, Sara salvaged what belongings she could from the water-soaked houseboat, got on a bus and left.

Not long afterward, while she was still at her mother's, the divorce papers arrived. She now reminded Morgan of those papers.

"Do you still have them?" he asked.

"I don't know where they are. I didn't have them framed," she added tartly, determined not to let him know how much their arrival had hurt.

She'd barely glanced at the papers when they were delivered. One look was enough to burn the words at the top of the page into her brain forever: *In the Matter of the Dissolution of the Marriage of Morgan McKenzie, Petitioner, Sara McKenzie, Respondent...*

Then tears had blurred the words and she'd shoved the papers into a drawer and cried until she lost all track of time. Cried because she still loved him. Cried because it had never occurred to her that he'd divorce her. Cried because she'd expected him to race down to her mother's place in San Diego and tell her he couldn't live without her and everything was going to be different.

Cried, she thought now, because she was young and foolish and overly emotional. And why there were tears in her eyes at this moment she had no idea. She quickly blinked them back.

Briskly she said, "I don't really know what became of them. I left San Diego, and then my mother also moved not long afterward."

"Which made you rather difficult to locate," he commented.

The coffee was done. When she made no move to offer him any he opened cupboard doors until he found cups. He filled two cups and set one on the kitchen counter beside her.

"Still drinking it black, I presume?"

"No, I use cream now." To emphasize that she was a different person than the one he had known, she briskly opened the refrigerator and added a splash of milk to the coffee. Then she turned and faced him, cup held as a small barrier between them. "You still haven't explained your claim that we aren't divorced. You're procrastinating again."

"Another of my many flaws. There's quite a list of them, isn't there?" He made an exaggerated sigh. "Anyway, as I said, after you walked out I was very upset. I rushed to a lawyer and filed for divorce, or as it is legally termed, a dissolution of marriage. The papers you received were the original petition for the dissolution."

"And?"

"I was supposed to show up in court for the hearing on a particular day, but by then I was down in Arizona."

That figured. Morgan hadn't even been responsible enough to show up for his own divorce. Yet the full implication of what that meant didn't sink in until he went on.

"So when I didn't show up, and the lawyer never heard from me... and I didn't get his bill paid right away... the whole thing was just dropped."

"Dropped?" Sara repeated in dismay. *"Dropped?"*

"Surely you realized that if the action had been completed a final decree dissolving the marriage would have been issued."

She stared at him in shock as the truth got through to her. The papers she had received were merely a petition for divorce, not an actual divorce decree. No doubt she should have realized the enormous difference between the two.

Perhaps she would have realized it if she hadn't hurt too much to read beyond the top line. But she *hadn't* realized it.

He smiled cheerfully and poured himself another cup of coffee. "So, unless you have at some time divorced me, here we are, still that happy couple all America knows and loves, Mr. and Mrs. Morgan McKenzie."

## Chapter Three

Sara's hands shook so badly that coffee sloshed out of the cup. So it was true. She and Morgan were still legally married. And Brian was expecting her to marry him in the very near future. Afraid she'd drop the coffee cup, she set it down very carefully on the counter. Then she lashed out at him.

"Morgan, how could you do this? How could you walk off and leave something as important as a divorce just...just up in the air? As if it were no more important than quitting another job? And then not even tell me the action had been dropped—"

"Before you completely condemn me, will you give me a chance to explain?" He smiled appealingly. "Doesn't the condemned man always get a few last words?"

"Only in stories, I believe." None of which Morgan, in spite of all those grandiose claims of becoming a writer, had ever gotten around to writing. "Why didn't you let me know that the divorce action had been dropped? Didn't it ever occur to you that I might remarry? That I might unknowingly wind up a *bigamist?*''

''I guess I never really thought you'd want to marry anyone else,'' he admitted slowly. He paused to consider that statement. ''A rather optimistic and unrealistic attitude, I can now see. You're a warm and beautiful and loving woman. Of course you'd want to marry again. And have plenty of chances to do it.''

He looked a little stunned, like a man who had just been hit with a shocking revelation.

Sara felt a momentary crunch of guilt, as if she had done something underhanded and indecent in her relationship with Brian. Which she hadn't, of course. She'd thought she and Morgan were through, divorced, and she was simply trying to get on with her life. But if she and Morgan *weren't* through . . .

No, she would not fall into that quicksand trap.

''You never considered remarriage yourself?'' she challenged.

''Not seriously. By the time I got back from the lawyer I knew filing for the divorce had been a mistake, and I've known for all but the first few months of our separation that we were still married. And I did try to find you,'' he added, before she could jump on him again. ''I went to your mother's place in San Diego, but the people living in the house she'd been renting had never heard of either of you. The landlord had no idea where she'd gone. You'd both just disappeared. And we never had been able to keep track of your father, of course.''

''My mother married a navy officer and is now living in Japan. My father and his young wife went the opposite direction and live in London. I went back East for a while and then came here to visit a friend from college while I tried to figure out what to do with my life. I started working at Junque and Stuffe on a temporary basis, but when the elderly owner decided to sell she offered me a very good deal and I took it.''

"No wonder I couldn't find you the first time around."

"But you've found me now," Sara pointed out. "So it must not have been so difficult after all."

"I hired an agency that specializes in tracking down people, and it took even them a couple of months to get a current address for you."

Sara was reluctantly curious about what he'd been doing during the past three years, but she didn't ask. The fact that he was wandering around the country on a bicycle was evidence enough that he hadn't changed his ways and undoubtedly had a new series of weird and peculiar jobs to add to his collection.

"Not being able to find you hit me hard. Damned hard." He sounded almost grim as he stared down at the coffee cup. "It got through to me that maybe I'd really lost you, that the fact that we were still married didn't mean much if I didn't have you. It made me step back and take stock of myself and where my life was going."

"I did a little stocktaking, too," she said. Rather pointedly she added, "I now have a credit card. Three, in fact. I own this." Her gesture took in the store and living quarters, not grand, but adequate. "I don't wonder where my next meal is coming from."

"I'm impressed," he agreed. "Would it impress you if I told you that I finished up those college credits I was lacking and got my degree?"

Yes, that information did impress Sara. She had done nothing further with her own education. But, given his current questionable circumstances, all she said was a cautious, "I'm pleased to hear that."

"Sara, what do you think caused us to split up?" Morgan asked. He leaned against the kitchen counter and surveyed her with thoughtful dark eyes.

Sara's answer was prompt. "Money. Or, to be more accurate, the lack thereof." She kept her eyes away from the tanned strip of bare skin running from his throat to his belt buckle. She remembered a foolish little walking-fingers game they used to play...

"Really?" He sounded dismayed. "That's why you're planning to marry Brian, because he has money? You think money is the basis of happiness?"

"Of course not! That's a...a terrible thing to say. It's insulting. As if you think I'm some sort of mercenary gold digger!"

"I'm sorry. I didn't mean it that way. I just didn't realize that you considered money the only problem in our marriage."

"Morgan, we were usually so broke that I saved pieces of plastic wrap to use again! I rationed out the dental floss. I made meatloaf that was all loaf and no meat. I tried to cut your hair with a pair of manicure scissors so you could apply for a job." Picturing the awful results of her efforts made her laugh. "And you wound up looking as if you'd been attacked by a pack of homicidal elves."

She cut the laugh short. She was not going to get into some foolish reminiscing session with him. She just repeated, "Money was our big problem."

"Okay, we were short of money," he agreed. "But deeper than that was the fact that we were both just too immature. We may have been old enough in years for marriage, as old as many couples who make their marriages work, but we were basically much too immature for marriage. We both had a lot of growing up to do. I had never learned to stick with anything. You were lost and confused about the breakup of your parents' marriage—"

"*We* were immature?" Sara interjected with deliberately heavy emphasis. "*I* was not the one who got fired because I overslept three days in a row or asked for a day off to go scuba diving after I'd been working only four days. I wasn't the one who traded our broken-down old car for an even more broken-down old motorcycle for the air-headed reason that with a different mode of transportation we'd meet new and different types of characters you could use in your books. I wasn't—''

"You're saying that you, of course, were completely mature and responsible? You call getting mad at me because I remarked that changing your hair color to bright red wasn't too flattering—''

"You told me I looked as if someone had dumped a plate of spaghetti sauce on my head!''

"But was climbing a tree and sitting there all night really a mature response to my remark?'' he asked.

"Was your threat to cut the tree down a responsible re-action?'' she retorted.

"I didn't actually start sawing,'' he protested, but he grinned guiltily.

She started to smile back but then caught herself and briskly rinsed her coffee cup instead. She reminded herself again that getting into old times could be dangerous. It could be all too easy to romanticize the past instead of re-membering the hard realities.

"I'm not trying to put blame anywhere,'' Morgan went on. "I'm just saying we were both immature. My running to a lawyer as soon as you walked out was immature. So was my not showing up for the divorce hearing. Although, un-der the circumstances, that may have been one of those lovely old blessings in disguise. Probably my subconscious was trying to tell me something.''

"There really is no point in rehashing all this,'' Sara said. She glanced pointedly at her watch. "It's getting late—''

"But there is one point that is definitely worth rehash-ing,'' Morgan said. "And that is the fact that we really loved each other. I don't think that has changed.''

He took a step toward her, but she backed away.

"Of course it's changed! I'm engaged to Brian now. We announced it to his parents and friends tonight.''

"Do you love him?''

Sara hesitated. "If you're asking if I feel about him the way I felt about you when we were first married, the answer is no. But I've learned that the starry-eyed, unrealistic kind of first love we shared is not the foundation upon which to base a lifelong relationship."

"And I've come to realize that people who can't come right out and say 'Yes!' when asked if they love someone, who feel they have to explain their feelings, aren't all that much in love."

"And since when have you become such an expert on love?" Sara flared. She swallowed, then deliberately looked at her watch again. "It's late and I don't intend to stand here arguing the nuances of love with you. Apparently, your claim that we are still married is true. Now the question is, what are you going to do to correct the situation?"

Morgan leaned against the kitchen counter and crossed his long legs. He smiled affably. "I don't intend to do anything about it. I'm quite happy being married to you."

"But I'm planning to marry Brian!"

"So you've said. But you're married to me, so won't that make for an, umm, somewhat awkward situation?" Morgan inquired. "Think of the headlines: Glamorous Secondhand Store Owner Involved in Bigamy Scandal. Or perhaps Banker Shocked When Bride's Real Husband Accompanies Couple on Honeymoon. Perhaps we'd even make it to the tabloids with the burning question, How Many Partners Make a Marriage? I wonder if they still ask that potentially embarrassing question at wedding ceremonies, the one about whether anyone present knows any reason the marriage should not take place?"

He cocked his head thoughtfully, as if he was picturing himself righteously leaping up to announce his claim on her as she stood at the altar with Brian.

"Of course I can't marry Brian until the legal situation is taken care of, but it certainly isn't an insurmountable problem," Sara snapped. "I can divorce you easily enough."

"Then, if you want to be not married to me, that is exactly what you'll have to do." He smiled that easy, infuriating smile.

Unfortunately, her claim that she could divorce Morgan easily enough was not completely accurate. There were definitely complications, the first of which was having to tell Brian and his parents all this. They would, of course, be appalled.

Brian would quite possibly be very angry. He, who was always so *precise* about both business and personal affairs, wouldn't understand how she hadn't differentiated between an initial petition for a divorce and an actual final divorce decree. An omission which she reluctantly had to admit was rather immature on her part.

Brian had always been even-tempered with her, but she knew from roundabout talk that he could be quite short-tempered when things went wrong at the bank; he and his father apparently held widely differing opinions on running things there. And hearing that she was still married definitely sounded like something that could make him short-tempered even with her.

Would it, she wondered uneasily, be enough to make him call everything off? No, surely not. He wasn't wildly demonstrative, never gave her impulsive public kisses the way Morgan used to, seldom even held her hand in public, but he said he loved her. And he'd certainly proven it in the way he'd taken charge with his parents this evening.

He'd proven it in many other ways, as well. Their relationship was still young, almost a whirlwind courtship, in fact, but he'd made it plain he wanted to marry her almost from the start. They'd never had a serious quarrel, seldom argued about anything. They'd planned a stable, responsible life together. They would live in his condo for the first year, during which time they'd look around for a choice piece of land on which to build. They both thought two children would be ideal, with the first one arriving during their second year of marriage.

But he would definitely be extremely upset about this news, and she couldn't blame him. At the very least, the wedding would have to be postponed for some time. There would also be the inevitable whirlwind of gossip, and the Athertons felt about gossip as they did about loan defaults at the bank.

Then another thought occurred to Sara. She instantly rejected it as utterly unacceptable, but it sneaked right back.

Suppose they didn't tell Brian's parents about this awkward complication? *Suppose she didn't even tell Brian?* Suppose she just quietly filed for divorce and stalled the wedding plans until she was legally free?

No, tempting as that was, it wouldn't be right. Honesty was much too important.

Also, even if she guiltily left honesty out of it, she didn't see how such a scheme would be possible. The local weekly newspaper regularly printed a list of the courthouse records of all the divorces in the county. She wasn't certain the Athertons read the little newspaper, which mostly featured items about local bake sales and squabbles among the local city council members, but it would be her bad luck that one of Brian's parents would browse through it the day the listing of her divorce was published. And even if neither Brian nor his parents personally read the notice, others would, and the juicy gossip would eventually get to them.

How about filing for the divorce in some other county where the fact wouldn't come out in the local newspaper? But even if she did that, it was quite possible the Athertons would find out anyway. They had ties with professional people, lawyers and judges, all over the state. And if they and Brian found out she'd deliberately tried to conceal the whole mess, the situation could be doubly disastrous.

"Problems?" Morgan inquired pleasantly.

"There are a few details to work out."

"Sara, he isn't right for you. You'd be miserably unhappy with him."

"You don't know him. You don't even know anything about him, except for irrelevant gossip you picked up around town. So you can't possibly know whether he's right for me."

"But I can see you. Look at you."

Sara had no idea what he was talking about and had no intention of looking at herself, but he turned her around to face her shadowy reflection in the window over the kitchen sink. His hands were on her upper arms, and his eyes met hers in their faint reflections.

"The hairdo isn't you at all—"

Sara's hand flew to the sleekly plastered style. "What's wrong with my hair?"

"It's all stiff and rigid and severe, not you at all." Morgan touched the hairspray-coated line sweeping upward from her ear. "You're romantic softness, the touchable kind of hair a man loves to run his fingers through, tendrils and flowing mane..."

He pulled a strand of hair loose, twisting it around his finger and then letting it fall against her cheek. His fingers grazed her earlobe and his palm brushed her jaw. Her skin reacted strangely, a hot tingle, a cold shiver.

Brian had never shown any interest in running his fingers through her hair. Which suited her just fine. She turned away from their reflections in the window and brushed Morgan's hand aside. "Don't do that."

Determinedly she grabbed the loosened tendril and tucked it behind her ear. But as soon as she moved her hand away the tendril slithered forward and fell free again, curling gently against her cheek.

Morgan shook his head. "Brian tries to do the same thing to you that you've done to your hair, force you into some stiff, unnatural shape. And it isn't going to work any better with you than it does with your hair."

"My hair is fine." She ignored the treacherous tendril. "And so am I."

"And the perfume, that isn't you, either. A gift from Brian, I'd guess, something very expensive, something that he chose by price without ever giving a thought to whether it suited *you*."

Damn him! How had he known the expensive perfume was a gift from Brian, that she'd never have chosen something so heavy and musky for herself?

"If you don't like the way I smell," Sara suggested in a frosty tone, "I suggest you move farther away so my perfume won't bother you. In fact, I *insist* that you move away."

He smiled and touched the pulse point in her throat. "I like the way you smell just fine. It's Brian's perfume I'm not crazy about."

When he made no move to put space between them, she did. Unfortunately, that only trapped her in the corner beyond the coffeemaker, and Morgan swiftly followed her. With one arm he blocked her escape and with the other he swept the imprisoning combs and pins from her hair. It tumbled to her shoulders in a dark swirl.

Almost fiercely he ran his hands through the free-flowing mass. He lifted the strands and let them fall, the way a more materialistic man might run his hands through a long-lost treasure of golden coins. Then his hands tightened around the strands. He tilted her head back, fingers harsh in her hair but thumbs softly caressing her throat.

"That's you. Free. Natural. As if you've been walking in the wind."

She shook her head against the velvet cage of his hands. "No! I've changed. I like this perfume. I like my hair...*not* as if I've been walking in the wind."

"You're trying to be someone you aren't to please Brian and his parents."

It was perhaps true that she'd had to make a determined effort to fit into the Athertons' world...an effort that at this point still wasn't totally successful...but that didn't mean she was trying to be someone she wasn't.

His hands slid forward until they cupped her jaw. His thumbs moved up to her lips. He caressed the softly rounded curves, and her lips trembled under the sensuous touch. She tried to break away, but his body held her prisoner in the corner.

"Morgan, you have no right to break into my home and my life and act like this—"

"Act like what? As if I want to kiss you?" He smiled, rich firepoints of desire gleaming in his dark eyes. "Because I do want to."

She put her hands on his chest to push him away, but he caught them in his and raised them high over her head. Even though she was fully clothed, her body felt exposed to him. He made no move to touch her, even held the lean line of his body away from hers, but his mouth dipped to hers, warm and passionate, not so much demanding as sweetly seductive. She felt the remembered strength of his lips, the tantalizing probe and retreat of his tongue, the unspoken invitation to weld her body to his and kiss him back the way she had done so many times in the past.

The temptation to do just that was frighteningly powerful. It swept through her like a storm wind buffeting the coast, ripping at logic and good sense the way the winter wind ripped at signs and trees and windows.

With supreme force of will she held the wind back. Her breath quickened and her heartbeat raced, her eyes closed and her muscles quivered, but she dismissed the unwanted reactions as merely biological reflexes, the reaction of one healthy young body to another, no more indicative of personal feelings than the jerk of a knee to a doctor's tap. She loved *Brian*. She repeated the words to herself to drown out the throb of her pulse. *I love Brian.*

Morgan laughed softly. "You're trying so hard not to respond. The effort is truly admirable. But you're not succeeding."

"The only thing I'm apparently not succeeding in is convincing you that I don't want to make love with you—"

He blinked in an expression of wounded innocence, but his smile was slyly wicked. "Who said anything about making love? All I said was that I wanted to kiss you, but

you took it a big leap farther." Mischief danced in his eyes.
"I find that extremely meaningful—"

He transferred both her hands to the strong grip of one of
his, and the other hand slid boldly down her body. She had
the panicky feeling that he was going to sweep her up in his
arms, and the next thing she knew she'd be tumbling into
bed with him.

With furious determination she lifted one leg and brought
the high heel of her sandal down on the top of his foot. He
was now wearing heavy boots, and her action had no more
physical effect on him than a kitten's swipe at a baseball.

He did seem to get the point, however. His hand stopped
in midcaress and he looked shocked.

"I'm rushing things, aren't I?" He sounded honestly
contrite, but Sara was not about to soften.

"You are acting like an oversexed, woman-starved, over-
bearing, insensitive *clod!*"

He let go of her and took a step backward. As she
straightened her dress and ran her fingers through her hair
she moved to the center of the room. She felt totally disheveled, although her reflection in the dark pane of the
kitchen window showed nothing out of the ordinary.

"I'm sorry," Morgan said. "I should have given you
more time to get used to the idea that we're still husband and
wife."

"A legal entanglement, nothing more, I assure you," Sara
stated.

"You're still using the name McKenzie," he observed
thoughtfully. "Most women change back to their maiden
name these days."

"I would have, but it was just too much bother to change
everything. Driver's license, Social Security—" She
shrugged impatiently, as if the list went on and on, although at the moment she couldn't think of anything else.

"I don't think that was the real reason. I think you didn't
drop the name McKenzie because you still wanted to be Mrs.

Morgan McKenzie." He nodded as if confirming the thought to himself.

"That may have been true at the beginning," Sara conceded. "But it is no longer true. I am looking forward to becoming Mrs. Brian Atherton as soon as possible."

"Which is not going to be in the *immediate* future," he pointed out. "Not within the next few days anyway."

That was so obvious that she saw no point even in dignifying the remark by agreeing with him. She stepped toward the door to usher him out.

He ignored the open door. "We'll have plenty of time to discuss all this later, then. So, where should I sleep?" He peered around as if expecting she had a spare bed hidden in the cupboard somewhere.

Sara looked at him blankly. "What do you mean?"

"Given your current grumpy attitude, I'm apparently not going to be invited into your bed immediately. So where should I sleep?"

Unwilling to think that this question really meant what it sounded as if it meant, she could only repeat, "What do you mean?"

"The floor? The sofa? Rollaway bed you have hidden somewhere? I know there isn't a second bedroom, because I looked around a bit before my nap. I have my sleeping bag, of course. I brought the rest of my things in from the bicycle while you were at dinner."

The question did mean what she thought. He actually thought he was going to spend the night under her roof. She quickly straightened him out on that point.

"Then I suggest you take your things back out to your bicycle and be on your way."

"And go where?"

"There's a campground a few miles south on Highway 101." She didn't bother to point out that there were also three motels in town. He wouldn't have sufficient funds to stay in one of them, of course.

"You'd toss me out on a cold, dark, dangerous highway, with nothing but a bicycle for transportation and protection?" Morgan clapped a hand to his chest in feigned horror at her cruelty. "I could be attacked by dangerous wildlife, shanghaied for a life of slavery at sea, struck by a car or truck, set upon by muggers and robbers."

Sara clenched her teeth in frustration. The first two suggestions were melodramatically unlikely, but the last two weren't. The possibility of getting struck by a vehicle while riding a bicycle on a dark highway was all too real. Making the coastal highway ride from the Columbia River south to the California border was a popular trip among avid bicyclists, but they didn't do it at night. She no longer wanted to be married to Morgan, but neither did she want the responsibility for his early demise on a dark highway.

Reluctantly she said, "I suppose you could stay here tonight." She looked at her watch as she had already done several times. A good share of the night was, in fact, already gone. "But *only* tonight," she emphasized firmly.

He gave her what she hoped wasn't, but feared was, a cheerful we'll-see-about-that smile.

She emphasized the point again. "Tonight only. Then you will definitely have to leave."

"But where would I go?" He made it sound as if she were casting him adrift on the high seas without even a hint as to where the nearest desert island lay. He lifted his hands and managed a woebegone expression.

"Where did you come from?" She was reluctantly curious about that. Wandering around the country on a bicycle with a knapsack and sleeping bag seemed a rather slender mode of existence even for Morgan.

"Here and there."

"You're still just drifting around the country, then?"

"More or less."

That was Morgan, of course. Here and there, more or less, nothing settled or definite or solid. She had to wonder how long it had been since he'd had a real bed to sleep in, how regularly he ate, if he had any warm clothes, whether he ever saw a dentist—

No, she told herself firmly. Those were not her worries. Ex-husbands were not like stray cats, to be given a home when they wandered in cold and hungry.

Briskly she said, "The sofa in the living room makes out into a bed."

She led the way into her tiny living room and tossed the cushions aside. The sofa, when opened, took up most of the open space. The mattress already had sheets on it. She got a pillow and extra blankets from the hall closet.

"You're welcome to watch the TV, if you'd like." She pointed to the remote control on the coffee table, which had been shoved off to one side. "The bathroom is down the hall... but you already know that. Extra towels are in the hall closet. But you probably know that, too."

"What's getting-up time around here?"

"For you, the earlier the better. There's bacon and eggs or a choice of cereals for breakfast. And don't forget to take your bottle of champagne with you when you go."

And wasn't it just like him, she thought in exasperation, to spend some of his few dollars on an expensive bottle of champagne in a foolish, futile gesture to revive a lost romance?

"This is really what you want, Sara? For me just to walk out of your life and disappear?"

"I've built a new life for myself here. It doesn't include you."

"It could."

Again she asked the question that she had seemed to be asking all evening. "What's that supposed to mean?"

"It means that I can now see the need for a home base in life. That's part of the maturing process I've been through. You're looking at the new and improved Morgan McKenzie, the dependable, pays-his-bills, shows-up-on-time Morgan McKenzie. I want to put roots down here, with you. Maybe a little cabin for two on the beach..."

Sara shook her head ruefully. "Houses with beach frontage here don't cost anywhere near as much as they do in California, but you still can't buy them with small change." She fluffed the pillow briskly, putting an end to what was a rather ridiculous midnight discussion. "Good night."

He was unbuckling his belt when she turned and headed for the bedroom. She heard him in the bathroom while she was making her own bed, fluffing the imprint of his head out of her pillow. She waited until his steps faded down the hallway before slipping out to brush her teeth and wash. Upon returning she turned the lock on the bedroom door before she set the alarm on her clock radio and slid into bed.

She planned, once she was alone and in bed, to think things through logically and decide what she must do about a divorce.

Instead her mind kept drifting back to scenes of her life with Morgan.

Investing in a Thanksgiving turkey... so inexpensive and economical per pound!... and then discovering that one large turkey lasts two people *forever*. Turkey sandwiches, turkey salad, turkey loaf, hot turkey, cold turkey, creamed turkey. They finally began to call it "the Turkeyville Horror," the turkey that would not die.

Their Christmas present to each other, a gift-wrapped carburetor for their clunky old car.

Their brief job working for the eccentric old millionaire who, dining in solitary splendor amidst candlelight and crystal and china, insisted on eating everything, from mashed potatoes to chocolate mousse, in the form of a sandwich. And discovering that Jell-O sandwiches weren't all that bad...

Strange, with all the hardships they'd had, what she remembered most was the laughter.

The laughter and the passion...

She stopped herself before the memories in that area became too explicit. You couldn't live on laughter and passion. She'd been through this with herself before.

She doubted she could sleep with the worrisome complication Morgan had introduced into her life hanging over her, to say nothing of the fact that Morgan himself was sleeping only a few feet away, but sleep she did, sweetly, dreamlessly.

She drifted up from sleep on the scented waves of bacon cooking and coffee brewing. It was a marvelous feeling, rocking in that dreamy state between sleeping and waking, the scents deliciously inviting, the sounds of country music on the kitchen radio flowing down the hallway.

She came fully awake with a jump that rattled the tray on the nightstand beside her. The bedroom door was wide open, the scents of bacon and coffee much closer than the kitchen.

Morgan pulled back the drapes to let in morning sunshine. He was again barefoot and shirtless. The light gleamed on his smoothly tanned skin and hair still damp from a shower.

"Good morning." The two words sounded as intimate as if his head were beside hers on the pillow.

"Morgan, the door was locked on purpose to keep you *out—*"

"You mean you thought I might sneak in here under cover of darkness and force myself on you?" He shook his head reproachfully. He squatted down beside the bed, his eyes on a level with hers. "Sara, darlin', I have my faults, but that isn't one of them. I prefer happy cooperation to force, which, as I recall, was your usual reaction to my advances. When you weren't making advances of your own."

Sara started to stand up and tell him to get out, realized that a see-through red teddy wasn't the most appropriate attire for such an action, and pulled the covers up around her neck, instead. She didn't bother asking how he'd gotten through the locked door. He'd already explained about his lock-picking education. Which he was apparently making more use of than his college degree.

"See? I've merely brought you breakfast in bed. Bacon just the way you like it, scrambled eggs not too dry, toast with apricot-pineapple jam on the side, no butter." When she made no move to accept the breakfast he sighed. "Well, I'll just go back to the kitchen so you can enjoy your meal since you apparently intend to play terrified virgin as long as I'm here."

His lips touched her forehead in a chaste kiss, which she refused to acknowledge in any way. Her eyes followed him over the barrier of blankets as he blew her another kiss from the doorway.

She thought about ignoring the breakfast he had prepared, but it did smell good and she was hungry. Hopefully this was some sort of parting gesture, and he'd be gone by the time she got up.

The breakfast was good, Sara had to admit. He always could fry bacon better than she could. She never seemed able to hit that just-right point between too limp and too crisp.

After breakfast Sara showered and dressed in her usual workday outfit of jeans and T-shirt. She peered out the bedroom window but couldn't see to the back of the parking area to tell whether Morgan's bicycle was gone. It must be. There were no more sounds from the kitchen or tiny living room.

For a moment she had a peculiar let-down feeling. Perhaps subconsciously she had wondered if there was some chance Morgan had changed and turned into that mature Rock of Gibraltar he had never been. But no, he was as lacking in persistence as ever, even at winning his wife back. He'd still be flitting from place to place, job to job, perhaps eventually from wife to wife, when they were both old and gray.

That last thought gave her a moment's pang. Morgan with another wife... Then she concentrated on relief that he was gone. He had ridden in on his bicycle and churned her life as blithely as turning the switch on a hot tub, but now he was gone and she could start trying to figure out how to straighten out the mess.

She would have to tell Brian, of course. There was no getting around that unpleasant fact. He wouldn't *necessarily* be angry, she reminded herself. Certainly not unreasonable. She hoped. Sara tried to assure herself that given his sensible, responsible attitude, it was quite likely he would prove helpful in deciding how to handle this mess most discreetly. The only question was, how best to tell him?

She carried the breakfast tray to the kitchen, noting, as she peered into the living room, that the sofa had been closed and sheets and blankets neatly folded. Good. Another indication that Morgan was gone. But she found the door to the store unlocked, which was odd. She was always careful to follow Brian's instructions to lock it. He had strong doubts about the moral character of her customers.

"Fascinating variety of items you have here!" Morgan's head popped up from between aisles. He prowled along the cluttered shelves, brushing a fingertip over a piece of Depression glass, tinkling a wind chime of sea shells, trying on a fringed leather vest.

"I thought you'd gone." Sara walked past him to unlock the front door and change the sign from Closed to Open.

"It occurred to me that I'd be doing you a terrible disservice if I did that." He inspected a Coleman camp stove and accompanying lantern. "Where do you get all this stuff to sell in the store?"

"I go to garage sales and flea markets and auctions. People come in with individual items or sometimes even a whole houseful to sell."

"Do you ever have problems with people trying to sell you stolen goods?"

"That's one thing I have to be especially careful about. I keep extensive records about where I buy things and from whom. Sometimes the police will ask me to be on the lookout for certain stolen items that someone may try to sell." Then she realized that Morgan had expertly led her into an irrelevant detour around the subject that was far more important than where the junk and stuff that became Junque and Stuffe came from. "Why would your leaving be doing me a disservice?"

"It occurred to me that if I'm not around and easily available, divorcing me may be considerably more difficult. I don't know what all the regulations are, of course, but I'm sure there are delays and complications if the respondent can't be located to be served with the proper legal papers. My being close by could simplify things for you."

Sara had no idea whether what he said about possible complications was accurate or not. But whether or not it was, she wasn't convinced of his good intentions. "Forgive my suspicious nature," she said, "but somehow I doubt your noble motives."

He sighed and then grinned as if they were in some marvelous conspiracy. "You always could see right through me."

"And your real reason for not leaving as you promised—?"

"I made no such promise," he declared in the surprised tone of a righteous man wronged. "Just because you thought—"

The bell on the front door jangled as two customers came in, and Sara interrupted her conversation with Morgan to ask if she could help them find something. They were "just looking" so she went back to check on this latest complication from Morgan.

In a fierce whisper she said, "Now, since you didn't stay to help me get a divorce and thus uncomplicate this situation, why *did* you stay?"

"Because I love you. Because I have no intention of giving you up without a fight." He paused as if he were reconsidering that statement. "Actually, I have no intention of giving you up under any circumstances."

"What kind of fight?" Sara asked in dismay. She had visions of physical confrontations with Brian or legal skirmishes stretching out endlessly. Morgan's next words did not ease her worries.

"Whatever it takes."

The bell on the front door jangled as the door opened again. Morgan's eyes lit up with interest, but Sara's heart sank.

Brian.

Confrontation number one.

## Chapter Four

"Well, well! Look what we have here." Morgan watched Brian wind through the aisles toward Sara.

A rush of panic tightened Sara's chest. She could not, she simply could *not* just spring an introduction to Morgan on Brian without some preparatory explanation.

"Pretend you're a customer," she muttered to Morgan.

She half expected him to ignore the request, rush up to Brian, thrust out his hand and identify himself as her husband. But, after a moment's deliberation, he feigned interest in the rack of men's clothing.

She paused to stack pans on a shelf as she went to meet Brian. Secondhand shoppers often seemed to prefer a little clutter, but she always had an urge to rush around and straighten things up when Brian appeared. After they were married, perhaps she really would turn Junque and Stuffe into an antique store. They'd undoubtedly all feel more comfortable with it that way.

"Are you feeling better this morning?" Brian asked. His expensive slacks and sports jacket contrasted with Morgan's faded jeans and scruffy T-shirt.

"Yes, I'm fine. I don't know what was wrong with me last night. Just the excitement, perhaps." A little uneasily she added, "Have you talked to your parents this morning?" Sara had suspected that the Athertons' private reaction to the engagement might be more stormy than the restrained acceptance she had witnessed the previous evening.

Two fine lines formed between Brian's blond eyebrows. "My father has decided to postpone his retirement for another year."

"Because you're planning to marry me?" Sara gasped.

"What? Oh, no, of course not. No connection. He just hates to let go of any control at the bank. Which is damned frustrating, since his ideas and ways of doing things are more suited to the finger-counting than computer age."

With some annoyance Sara realized that Morgan was taking in every word Brian said. He was still loitering near the rack of men's clothing, openly eavesdropping. Brian, with his back to Morgan, apparently didn't realize how close Morgan was. Or perhaps he simply hadn't noticed Morgan. Brian tended to look right through people who wore old jeans and T-shirts with the picture of a motorcycle printed in fluorescent green on the back.

"It's only temporary, of course. He can't hold on forever." Brian dismissed the subject with a shrug of one shoulder. His voice dropped and turned more intimate. "If you're feeling better, perhaps we could run up to Portland for the weekend. We could find some romantic place to stay, pick out the ring together..." He brushed his fingertips lightly over her hand.

Sara, realizing Morgan was hearing every word of the intimate invitation, felt the pink of embarrassment rise to her cheeks. She unobtrusively retreated, pulling Brian with her, so they would be out of Morgan's range of hearing.

She also needed a few moments to think. She was in that corner again. Brian expected a more intimate relationship now. And perhaps she *should* go away with him for the weekend. It would certainly make plain to Morgan that Brian was the man in her life now.

But she hadn't time for more than a moment of uneasy indecision. Morgan barged up carrying a denim work shirt.

"Miss, could you tell me how much this shirt is?"

Sara shot him a withering look. She hadn't meant for him to play his role as customer quite so convincingly, as he well knew. "All the items are tagged with a price."

"I don't see a tag on this one."

Sara grabbed the shirt and pointed to a yellow price tag stuck to the sleeve.

"Oh. Thank you. That's very reasonable."

Sara waited until Morgan was putting the shirt back on the rack before murmuring to Brian. "A weekend in Portland sounds lovely, but—" She floundered for a reasonable "but."

Morgan came back, this time carrying a heavy jacket. "Would you happen to know if the filling of this jacket is goose down?" His face was all innocence, just as if he were a normal customer with no inkling that he was interrupting a very private conversation.

"I have no idea," Sara snapped. "But you're welcome to step outside and see if any of the local geese salute it."

Sara saw the amazement on Brian's face. "Perhaps I'm a little on edge today," she murmured by way of apology. Apology to Brian, *not* to Morgan, whom she knew was deliberately trying to sabotage her conversation with Brian. Brian, she noted, was definitely seeing Morgan now, looking beyond the unimpressive clothing to the rugged good looks and lean physique.

Brian, after a brief frown, turned back to Sara, putting himself between her and Morgan. Still in an intimately lowered voice he said, "All the more reason to get away for a couple of days. Couldn't you call that woman who works part-time for you? Or just close up for the day?''

Morgan hadn't had the courtesy to move away, but Sara forgot his presence for a moment. This was a point she and Brian had discussed before, the only point on which they had come close to an argument.

"Anne can't come in until after lunch today. And I can't just close up and leave. This is a business establishment. Summer weekends are my busiest and most profitable time.''

Brian smiled. "I don't think the bank is going to foreclose on your mortgage. I understand the local banker is a *very* understanding man." His hand squeezed the small of her back, massaging lightly.

For a moment Sara resented his teasing attitude. He always acted as if Junque and Stuffe were just some toy she could play with in her spare time. But then she realized he was merely trying to keep a minor disagreement from escalating into an argument, and she had to appreciate that sensible attitude. She also didn't want to get into anything with him in front of Morgan. And added to that was the more important problem of what to do with his weekend invitation.

Morgan, who had apparently seen the intimate gesture and didn't like it, interrupted again.

This time he had figured out something that would take longer than the answer to a simple question. "Oh, Miss, could you show me how this stove works?''

About the same time a trio of small motor homes pulled up outside and she could see the occupants heading for the door of the shop.

"I just can't get away today," Sara said to Brian. She motioned toward Morgan and the other customers by way of explanation. "It looks as if it's going to be a busy day. But perhaps this evening—''

"I'll probably run up to Portland by myself, then, and stay overnight. I want to get in a few more rounds of golf with the man who is considering building the shopping center here.'' Brian rolled his eyes slightly. ''My father, as you might guess, feels the development is too risky for the bank to get involved in and is against the whole thing.''

''That's...unfortunate,'' Sara said somewhat lamely, because at the moment she was rather grateful for Brian's disagreement with his father. It distracted him from being unhappy with *her*. She was also all too aware of Morgan's listening ears.

Brian leaned over and gave her a discreet kiss on the corner of the mouth. ''I'll call or come by when I get back tomorrow.''

When Brian walked out, Morgan abandoned his phony interest in the stove. He came around the end of the aisle and together they watched Brian's convertible pull out of the parking lot.

''Interesting,'' Morgan murmured. He nodded sagely. ''Very interesting.''

People were wandering all over the store, people to whom she should be giving her attention, but there was something disquieting about Morgan's enigmatic comment. ''What do you mean, 'interesting'?'' she demanded in a whisper.

''Your dearly beloved fiancé invites you to spend a romantic weekend with him. He even invites you to help pick out the engagement ring. And you turn him down flat. Did you do it because I'm here?''

''Of course not. Don't be so egotistical. I simply can't get away from the store just now—''

To prove it, she hurried over to a customer who was examining one of her more expensive items, a coffee table made from a polished slab of redwood. A moment later she victoriously rang up the good sale, along with purchases by two of the women who'd bought some graceful old bottles. Morgan helped carry out the coffee table and fit it into the compact motor home.

''Thank you,'' she said stiffly when he returned. She didn't like owing him for even that small favor. She ener-

getically dusted the counter by the cash register, hoping he
wouldn't get back to the subject of her turning down Brian's
weekend invitation. No such luck, of course.

"But you do take weekend trips with him," Morgan said,
just as if the previous conversation hadn't been interrupted.

"That's none of your business."

She whipped the dustcloth over the shelf of small appli-
ances, toasters and blenders and waffle irons.

Morgan grabbed her arm and turned her around to face
him. He scrutinized her face as if he were an artist planning
to paint her. Then he said, "I was wrong. You don't take
weekend trips with him." Suddenly a big grin flashed across
his face. "You've never even made love with him!"

"Morgan, for heaven's sake . . . Brian and I are engaged
to be *married*." She jerked away and attacked a harmless
microwave oven as if it were a major menace to society.

"You haven't, have you?" It was gleeful statement more
than question.

She refused to look at him and moved on to straighten the
mismatched silverware in a plastic tray. Coldly she repeated her earlier statement. "My personal life is none of
your business."

"I don't know the reasons you've given yourself, of
course, but I know the *real* one."

Sara knew the reason perfectly well. She'd had inner di-
alogues with herself about it. Her relationship with Brian
had been something of a whirlwind courtship, and, after the
failure of a marriage, she was naturally reluctant to rush too
soon into physical intimacy with someone else.

"And your interpretation of the real reason is—?" She
asked the question solely because she intended to point out
the error of whatever answer he gave.

"That you're still in love with me, of course." Morgan
beamed like the proud recipient of some major trophy.

Too late Sara realized that she had made a mistake, that
her question merely confirmed his suspicions about the ab-

sence of a physical relationship between her and Brian. She gave up her pretense of busyness and turned to confront him.

"Morgan, you are living in some private little fantasy world. Come out of it and face facts. The marriage between you and me is over, and, whatever may or may not have taken place between Brian and me, I *am* going to marry him."

But now it was Morgan who was suddenly very busy. "You know, that old trunk and the glass fishing float in the net would make a marvelous window display. Along with that painting of the seacoast and maybe that cast-iron pot off to one side, with a few of those silk flowers in it—"

"Help yourself," Sara muttered. He obviously wasn't leaving, so he might as well make himself useful.

Morgan spent most of the morning working on the window display. Business was brisk. Sara reluctantly suspected that having a handsome hunk working in the window that faced the street didn't exactly hurt business. Single-looking young women were not her usual customers, but several of them came in this day. They all found some reason to say something flirtatious to Morgan, and he flirted right back, of course. But, apparently feeling they had to justify having come in, they usually bought something. Morgan sold the seacoast painting he was putting in the display to one woman. Another girl, attention focused on Morgan, bought a couple of silvery fishing lures that Sara suspected the girl absentmindedly thought were earrings. She'd better not get her face too close to the water when wearing them, Sara thought a bit grumpily.

The window display, Sara had to admit when Morgan was finished, was quite attractive. But then, why wouldn't it be? Another of his short-lived careers had been with a firm that did window decorating for small businesses.

Sara usually just grabbed a carton of yogurt and an apple or orange for lunch, but Morgan, after waiting on a couple of customers while she was busy with another, disappeared into the living quarters and came back a few minutes later with sandwiches and coffee. He picked up a couple of bar stools from her furniture section and stationed them cozily side by side at the cash register counter.

"So, now that Brian is going to be gone and you are...ah...unencumbered for the evening, what are we going to do?" he asked conversationally between chomps of his sandwich. "Romantic walk on the beach? A stroll down to the park for a bit of people-watching? Or I could take you for a nice ride on my bicycle."

Sara refused to acknowledge the appeal of his whimsical suggestions or to give more than a quick thought to the free fun they used to have just sitting on a park bench making up wild stories about people who passed by. She scooted her stool away from his.

"*We* aren't going to do anything. *You,* unless you want to find yourself sleeping alongside the road tonight, had best load your gear and get out to the campground before it's full."

Sara expected an argument, but Morgan just gave a melodramatic sigh and finished his sandwich. Anne Cassidy, her part-time clerk, arrived right after lunch. While Sara was asking about Anne's husband, who was recuperating from a serious logging accident in the woods, Morgan disappeared. Later, when there were no customers in the store, she made a quick tour of her living quarters. Morgan's knapsack and other meager belongings, along with the bicycle, were gone.

She felt a twinge of regret and another of guilt. She brushed off the regret, but the guilt was a matter of business. She should have paid him for his morning's work. It would have been a way to help him without having him think any personal feelings or concern for his welfare were involved. Because personal feelings were *not* involved, of course.

Then she opened the refrigerator and found one item he hadn't taken with him. The champagne. Suddenly she was angry with him all over again. He was no doubt doing without something much more important... food? a space at the campground?... all because he'd foolishly spent the money on that champagne.

After closing the store she intended to catch up on some bookkeeping, but both office and living quarters seemed unnaturally quiet and empty. She turned on the radio but the impersonal noise only emphasized the emptiness. She thought about taking a walk on the beach, which she often did after work, but that held no appeal, either, on this particular evening.

At about seven-thirty she decided on impulse to drive out to the campground and make certain Morgan actually had a place to stay. On a second impulse she grabbed a used one-man pup tent off a shelf. Clouds had blown in and a wind was coming up. He'd need more than a sleeping bag for camping on the coast tonight. It would also be a convenient opportunity to return his champagne to him.

Her battered old pickup coughed and sputtered when she turned the key, and the engine had an ominous-sounding growl for the first mile or so on the road. She was going to have to buy a different pickup one of these days. Brian wanted her to buy a new one...he'd smilingly offered bank financing at very favorable terms... but she suspected that she got better deals when buying secondhand merchandise for the store if she didn't look too prosperous.

She stopped at the entrance gate to the campground and inquired if a Morgan McKenzie had registered. "Tall, dark-haired guy riding a bicycle, blue knapsack—?"

The busy gate attendant indicated a stack of registration forms. "I don't have time to look for the name, but if he's here he'd be assigned to the tent section down by the beach."

"Thanks. I'll see if I can find him."

Sara drove slowly through the campground, easing the old pickup carefully over the speed bumps. Most of the spaces were filled, everything from modest pickup-mounted campers to travel trailers, fifth-wheels with tipouts and luxurious motor homes. The tent area was almost empty, however. Sara didn't see Morgan or his bicycle as she drove by. She parked the pickup and made another quick tour on foot.

No Morgan.

Good, she told herself briskly. That meant he must have gotten on his bicycle and just ridden off into the sunset. Fine. He wasn't her responsibility anyway. Except she did have this worrisome vision of him plugging along the winding coast road in the dark...

She got in the pickup and headed back toward the check-in area. Wind scudded a paper plate across the road. Then Sara slammed on the brakes. There he was, bicycling toward her as if he hadn't a care in the world. Flanked by two long-legged blondes who looked as if they probably made workout videos in their spare time.

He also skidded brakes when he saw her. He dismounted and wheeled the bicycle up to her window. He waved the blondes on by with a casual, "See you later." Sara, for no particular reason, glared at them.

"The Simonson twins," Morgan said, as if that explained something. "And what are you doing here?" he added.

Good question, she realized uneasily. What *was* she doing here?

He grinned. "Not that I object, of course. I'm delighted. But given your less-than-enthusiastic response to my presence at Junque and Stuffe—"

"I had this old pup tent that's been sitting around for a long time. I haven't been able to sell it, so I thought you might as well have it. It could rain tonight. And I brought the champagne that you left in the refrigerator."

"I'm touched by your concern for my welfare." He dipped his head and flung a hand to his chest in a melodramatic display of gratitude, but Sara heard a hint of seriousness in the words.

Not that he needed the tent, she decided sourly. The blondes would probably be delighted to take in a ruggedly good-looking, carefree guy with a bicycle...and a grin that combined little-boy charm with a dangerously appealing sexiness.

"I just rode up to the store to buy some wieners and buns. I'm having a wiener roast on the beach. How about joining us? My new friends are bringing soft drinks and a kite to play with." He smiled again.

Morgan, a kite and a harem of two blondes and her cozily roasting hot dogs on the beach. No, thanks.

"I dropped my sleeping bag and knapsack back there." Morgan waved in the general direction from which she had come. "I'll pick them up and meet you in the tenting area, okay?" He raced off without giving her a chance to reject the invitation.

Sara selected a good spot for the pup tent, only a few feet from the sandy beach but with a narrow strip of trees and brush for shelter from the wind. She tossed the plastic-wrapped tent on the ground and set the bottle of champagne on top of it. When Morgan still hadn't returned after several minutes she decided she may as well set up the tent.

"Hey, thanks! That looks terrific," Morgan said when he arrived. He dumped his sleeping bag and knapsack inside the small, triangular-shaped tent. "And here come my new friends now."

"I'll be going, then—" Sara turned, expecting to see the blond bookends, but instead found a young couple and two small boys carrying a menacing-looking black, batwing kite. Her unexpected feeling of relief annoyed her.

"Sara, these are the Cannons, Doug and Jennifer, and that's Mike and that's Dave," Morgan said as he pointed to the pair. He always could walk into a roomful of strangers and have new friends in five minutes. "Everyone, this is my—this is Sara," he amended, apparently deciding to forgo complicated details.

The Cannons looked curious, and the woman sneaked a speculative look at the pup tent, but they didn't ask questions.

"It's supposed to swoop and dive like a big bat," the older boy explained about the kite. "But when we try to make it do tricks all it does is smash into the ground."

"Like a dead duck," the smaller boy added gloomily.

"And neither of us have had any better luck with it," Doug Cannon added.

"I don't know much about kites that behave like dead ducks," Morgan said, "but Sara worked in a kite shop for a while?" He gave her a questioning glance.

Sara had had her share of unlikely jobs, too. One had involved giving demonstrations of the stunt kites sold by the shop where she was working.

She looked at the boys and the kite. She should go. Just tell Morgan, "You're welcome," for the tent, jump in her pickup and head for home. There was danger here. She wasn't certain what it was, but it was here, as plain as the raw scent of the ocean and the cry of sea gulls. She shouldn't risk even this minor bit of involvement with Morgan. She should be at home. Waiting for Brian to call.

But it had been a long time, a long, long time, since she'd flown a kite on the beach or roasted hot dogs over a campfire...

And what could possibly go wrong with a pleasant couple and their two kite-flying little boys as chaperons?

"I might see if I could make it work," Sara said cautiously.

Moments later she had the kite in the air. Wind tossed her hair into a tangled froth, but the steady breeze was just right for kite-flying. Using the two handles, she drew on long-unused skills to make the stunt kite loop and dive and figure eight. She'd almost forgotten how much fun kite-flying was. She laughed joyously, and so did the boys. She showed them how to manipulate the handles to make the kite do stunts, and then they were even more delighted.

She felt invigorated and a little breathless as she stood with Morgan and watched the boys and the kite. They hadn't perfected the stunts yet, but they were keeping the kite in the air and having a glorious time racing along the beach. The parents draped their arms around each other as they watched their boys, and Sara felt a small pang of envy. Then she realized that Morgan wasn't watching boys or kite; his eyes were on her, warm and tender.

"Does it ever occur to you that if things had gone differently we might have a little kite-flier of our own by now?"

Sara swallowed. She'd momentarily had that same thought. But children couldn't exist on wild dreams and flyaway plans. They needed a secure home and bed and regular meals. But she chose to ignore the question rather than get into some irrelevant argument. "You could have helped the boys with the kite," she said. "You didn't need me to do it."

"I suppose I could have," he admitted. "But you looked as if you really needed a little kite-flying." He grinned.

"And I suppose I look as if I need a wiener roast, too?"

"Oh yes, definitely." Morgan nodded knowingly. "You need a wiener roast even more than kite-flying. You may just shrivel up and blow away if you don't have a wiener roast soon. Brian doesn't go in for such foolishness, of course."

Sara refused to confirm or deny the accuracy of that statement. She wasn't staying for any wiener roast, she decided. No way. She could already see other ideas spinning around in Morgan's head. Intimate, after-the-wiener-roast-when-the-chaperons-are-gone ideas. But she would go home, fix some soup and salad and wait for Brian's call.

A wail from the beach made them both look in that direction.

"Oh-oh," the boys' father said. "Disaster."

In his excitement the smaller boy had stumbled over a chunk of driftwood and dropped the handles. Now the kite merrily danced higher and higher until it was just a black dot disappearing over the trees. The boys returned with disappointed faces. Morgan tousled the younger one's hair in silent comfort.

"Can we go find it?" the older boy asked.

"I'm afraid it's headed for kite heaven now," Morgan said. "But I'll see if I can find another one for you tomorrow, okay?"

"Morgan, those stunt kites are expensive," Sara murmured. "You shouldn't get the boys' hopes up when you can't afford to buy—"

"But we still have hot dogs!" Morgan interrupted. "So let's get some driftwood and get the campfire going."

Sara was out gathering driftwood with the others before she realized that her smart intention of leaving had somehow been sidetracked. Okay, she'd stay a few minutes longer, but just until they got the campfire going. The wind was stronger now, flurries of sand dancing along the beach, and the clouds had darkened.

Morgan had the campfire blazing in moments. "We ought to let it die down to embers for the best wiener roasting," he told the boys, "but it's getting dark and looks like rain so maybe we'd better just get started, okay?"

And just about the time Sara thought, *now I really am going,* the scent of sizzling wieners stopped her short. The smell worked like an anchor on her feet and a magnet on her stomach. She took deep, hungry breaths, feeling as if she hadn't tasted a roasted wiener in centuries.

"The lady gets the first one." Morgan bowed elaborately as he presented her with a mustard-slathered wiener in a bun.

Wieners, she reminded herself, were full of cholesterol and all sorts of other unpleasant things...

The wiener crunched when she bit into it. It was burned to a blackened crust outside, lukewarm inside. The bun had Morgan's fingerprints squashed in it. Mustard and juices dripped down her chin.

And no fancy restaurant dinner had ever tasted better. Sara relished every bite and licked her fingers. Then, aware that after the first one it was every man, woman and boy for himself in the wiener arena, she impaled two on a forked stick. A few scattered raindrops were falling, the fire sputtering where they hit, but the boys' enthusiasm was undampened. They inhaled wieners like a couple of stray puppies.

"Wish we had marshmallows," the older boy said.

"Hey, I think I have some back at—" Morgan broke off. "I mean I had some back at the store but I guess I forgot to get them."

Finally Jennifer Cannon said, "C'mon, kids. Time to get ready for bed. I'm sure Morgan and Sara have... other things to do."

The woman's second speculative glance at the tiny tent made Sara jump up and make going-away motions of her own.

The boys responded with the inevitable groans and pleadings for a few more minutes, but their mother was firm. Nature apparently decided to take her side, because the scattering raindrops suddenly turned to a downpour. The couple snatched up their sons and raced off with friendly yells about seeing Morgan tomorrow.

Morgan grabbed Sara's hand, pulled the flap of the tent aside and shoved her toward the opening.

"Hey, I don't want to—" she protested, but another shove sent her sprawling into the tiny tent.

"No point in getting wet. The rain may not last more than a few minutes."

Morgan crowded in behind her, filling the tiny triangle with his lean frame. Sara couldn't see a thing. The pup tent was barely high enough to sit up in. There seemed an overabundance of arms and legs and bodies in the cramped space. Scents of smoke and damp clothes and hair filled the air.

Unexpectedly Sara felt Morgan's hands on her shoulders and his face against her hair. He breathed deeply. "Now there is a perfume I like," he declared.

She wrestled out of his grasp. "Morgan, I want out of here—"

"The rain is coming down even harder now. You'll get soaked if you try to get to the pickup."

The pickup was where she should have gone in the first place, Sara realized, but it was a little late now.

"I'll just get the sleeping bag rolled out so it's a little more comfortable in here. Then we can lie here all snug and cozy and listen to the storm."

More squirming and twisting, colliding of bodies, tangling of legs. Hands touching unintended places. At least when Sara's hands encountered unknown body parts it was unintentional; she wasn't so certain about Morgan's touches. His hands seemed to have an unerring radar for finding intimate points. Another scent was added to the damp, smoky smells of hair and clothes, the not-unpleasing aroma of warm male body. Suddenly Sara felt surprisingly warm, too. And she wasn't certain the warmth came just from physical exertion in the cramped space. She resisted an urge to remove her light jacket.

Finally Morgan got the sleeping bag spread out and the lumpy knapsack shoved to the foot end of the tent. He stretched out on his stomach and pushed a corner of the flap aside. Outside, the campfire sizzled and spit, flames dying to smoky wisps under the onslaught. The rain pounded down harder than ever, hitting the nylon tent like battering pellets.

"Maybe I was wrong. Sounds as if it might be settling in to pour down all night." Morgan sounded cheerfully pleased with that possibility. He zipped the tent flaps together. "Want to get inside the sleeping bag? It would be more comfortable."

Sara remained in a cross-legged sitting position. She straightened her back stiffly. "No, thank you. I'm quite comfortable now."

Morgan fumbled with a lump between them. "What's this? Oh, the champagne. Terrific! I'd forgotten you'd brought it. Shall we open it?"

*"No, thank you!"* The last thing she needed was the giddy, heady feeling champagne usually gave her. She needed to keep all her thoughts and senses under tight control in this situation.

A car drove by slowly, headlights momentarily illuminating the interior of the tent. Morgan was on his side, head braced on his hand. His hair fell across his forehead in rakish disarray, but his expression was oddly pensive.

"You had fun this evening, didn't you?" he asked softly.

Sara murmured something noncommittal, but inwardly she had to admit that, yes, she'd had fun. Brian wasn't a kite-flying, wiener-roast kind of person, and sometimes she did miss that sort of thing. But he had many other far more important qualities. He was hardworking and dependable, consistent and responsible. The future with him stretched out firm and secure. And they had fun together, too, she reminded herself. Dinners at good restaurants...he was very knowledgeable about food and wine. Dancing...he was a marvelous dancer. They both liked tennis and jazz and spy movies.

And while she was determinedly reminding herself of all Brian's good qualities Morgan was pulling her down beside him on the sleeping bag.

"I've missed you, Sara," he whispered huskily. "You don't know how much. For over three years I've dreamed about holding you again..."

His fingertips roamed her face, delicately brushing her eyebrows and lips, caressing the curve of her cheek and temple and tracing the fragile bridge of her nose. Each fingertip left a flickering trail of sparks behind it.

"After three years you're more beautiful than ever."

The fingertips trailed around her ear and down her throat, sweet as a first kiss, sensuous as a first intimacy. And tempting, oh, so tempting...

Sara held herself very still, thinking she shouldn't let him do this, she *mustn't* let him do this . . . and in just a moment she'd stop him. She really would, just as soon as—

And then the time limit went a little hazy as she fought an urge to do to him what he was doing to her. To see him through her fingertips, explore the remembered hollows and planes of his face . . . the almost invisible little irregularity of his nose, souvenir of a childhood bicycle accident; the clean softness of freshly shaven cheek, the sensuous curve of ear-lobe, the bony ridge beneath his eyebrows. Did that little section of his left eyebrow still grow at a rebellious angle?

Her fingers hovered over his face, longing, too, to investigate the unfamiliar crescent of the scar on his jaw, but she drew her hand back sharply before it could touch him. Touches were a definite danger area.

"Sara, are you ever sorry you walked out on me?"

She clasped her hands together to keep them from wandering. "I've considered that it might not have been the best . . . solution to our problems. But that was a long time ago," she added firmly. "Things are different now."

"One thing isn't any different. I still love you." He laughed softly. "Remember that old walking-fingers game we used to play?"

His hand went to the zipper of her jacket, but she blocked the downward motion of the zipper before it got to the valley between her breasts. Yes, she remembered the silly game. All too well. Inquisitive fingers strolling across her body, climbing a winding trail to the peak of her breasts, wandering to investigate the architecture of her navel, all the time accompanied by a tour guide narrative.

"And this, ladies and gentlemen," Morgan would say, "is the hip, generally regarded as the most beautiful hip in the world. Note the sensuous curve, and especially note this ticklish spot right here . . ."

And then the walking-fingers would wander lower and lower until the game was forgotten in an overflow of passion.

The atmosphere inside the tiny tent, in spite of the cold rain battering the exterior, suddenly felt almost steamy. Sara felt the warmth of his breath on her ear, but an ever-greater heat rose from within her.

"Kiss me, Sara," he whispered.

"No—"

And then his mouth was on hers, his lips warm and tender but at the same time fiercely possessive. She felt the hunger in him and in herself. Memories washed over her...memories of past intimacies, memories of making love and being in love, memories of tangled bodies and entwined souls, memories of one of them asking, "How long will you love me?" and the other one answering, "Forever 'n' ever," and it didn't matter who did the asking and who did the answering because they were one.

Yet there was more than memories. There was the here-and-now magic of lips that were soft yet so strong, tongue that was both tender and fiery, hand slipping beneath jacket and blouse to find warm skin. He made a noise, part groan of yearning, part murmur of satisfaction, as his hand found the curve of her breast and cupped it with gentle strength.

She kissed him back, wrapping her arms around him, making small murmurs of her own, smelling mingled scents of sea and smoke and him, tasting the flavor of mouth that was uniquely his own. One hand slipped into the damp thickness of his hair, the other dipped beneath the opening of his old T-shirt and found the smooth muscles tapering from neck to shoulder.

His body pressed closer, and his arms drew her against the full length of him as they lay on their sides. He wrapped a leg around her, and his kiss deepened.

And all her sensible thoughts whirled away, dancing on the wind of longing, until, like the flyaway kite, they were mere specks in the distance...

# *Chapter Five*

Something plopped on Sara's closed left eyelid. She moved her head without breaking the kiss. The next cold drop hit her temple.

She opened her eyes and stretched her right hand toward the edge of the tent. She still couldn't see anything, but she could feel it. Water. Puddles of it.

"Morgan, I think the tent is leaking." Outside, wind-whipped rain still hammered the tent, but now it felt as if a minor drizzle was also starting *inside* the tent. Morgan's hair was no longer merely damp; drops of water beaded the crisp strands. "Can't you feel the water dripping on your head?"

Morgan laughed softly. "Sweet Sara, all I can feel is you in my arms and how much I want you. I've waited over three years for this, and it's going to take more than a few rain-drops and a leaky tent to distract me."

Her jacket and blouse were open now. Morgan dipped his mouth to the curve of her breast, and for a few moments she, too, forgot the mini-tide rising around them in the greater tide of their need for each other. She cradled his head in her hands as his kisses awakened sweet memories and fresh desires. He ran a fingertip over the lacy seam of her bra and then reached both hands behind her back to unfasten the hooks, his hands fumbling in rough urgency.

Sara arched her upper body to help him. And stuck her elbow in a cold puddle that felt large enough to float a battleship.

"It isn't just a few raindrops! Either the tent has holes or it's just so old that it isn't waterproof anymore."

At least on top. The floor of the tent appeared to be holding water just fine. The puddles were uniting to form a lake, with water already squishing up through the sleeping bag. Morgan, his body half over hers, just murmured something soothing and nuzzled her throat as if they were entwined on a bed of the finest satin sheets.

"Morgan, I'm getting *soaked*. In a few more minutes, we're going to need a life raft in here."

"Sara, darlin', *I* am your life raft," he stated with noble magnanimity.

Morgan rolled over on his back, deftly lifting her body on top of his. He wrapped his long legs around her...and then gave a surprised yelp as cold water hit some vital area. "Hey, we've got a flood in here!"

"That's what I've been trying to tell you."

More tangles of arms and legs and bodies as Morgan crawled around trying to locate the source of the problem, this time with the added complication of a small mountain of soggy sleeping bag in the middle of the tent. Sara, also soggy, sat on a corner of the mountain, confused by the emotions sloshing around inside her like driftwood on a choppy sea.

She should feel relieved. She *did* feel relieved. If this tent-sized version of the Johnstown Flood hadn't happened she might very well have wound up making love with Morgan, but the romantic magic that had momentarily sizzled between them was safely waterlogged now. Yet mingled with the relief was a disturbing sense of loss and disappointment that she abruptly decided not to investigate too closely.

"Something's leaking all right," Morgan announced finally.

It was the understatement that got to her. Like his once saying, "We're a little short of money this week," when, on examination, they found that between them they had exactly ninety-seven cents and a coupon for a free bottle of mint-flavored mouthwash. And no credit card.

"I always wanted to try a water bed," he now added cheerfully, "but this isn't exactly what I had in mind."

The cheerfulness got to her, too. Or maybe it was pure frustration that made her lash out, because for a few reckless moments she'd desperately *wanted* to make love with him.

"Morgan, you haven't changed one bit! This is just like you. Totally disorganized. Completely irresponsible. Living like a . . . a traveling disaster area. Cold, wet—"

"Whoa, there, Sara, my love. I hate to sound unappreciative or picky about details, but this is *your* tent."

In the discomfort of squishy shoes, wet clothes and dripping hair, that small detail had slipped her mind.

In addition, they discovered when they crawled outside, she'd chosen a low spot on which to erect the tent, and rainwater from the surrounding higher ground had drained into it. Some rain had leaked through the top of the old tent, but the main source of the interior flood was that the tent was now a triangular island in a pool some three inches deep and ten feet across.

By the time they got the tent and Morgan's bicycle into the back of the pickup, they were even more thoroughly drenched. Sara's wet hair clung like seaweed to her head and neck. Water trickled down her back. And on top of that, when Sara turned the ignition key, nothing happened. The engine wouldn't start. Morgan had to get out in the rain again and do something under the hood to get it going.

While he was doing that Sara took off her jacket and wrung water from it onto floorboards that were also puddled because she'd left the windows open.

When they passed under the lights at the exit, he looked over at her and grinned with wicked appreciation. "And the winner of the wet T-shirt contest is—Sara McKenzie!"

Sara refused to dignify that with a comment.

The phone was ringing when Sara unlocked the door to her living quarters. She dripped her way across the kitchen to it.

"Sara, where have you been? I've been trying to call you for an hour. I was beginning to get worried."

"Brian, how sweet of you to be concerned. But everything's fine. I . . . just went down to the beach for a while. It started raining and I got soaked. I'm standing here dripping right now."

All true enough, although she guiltily knew that certain omitted details were perhaps more important than those she had included.

Brian went on to tell her how well his golfing afternoon with the developer had gone. Then his tone turned intimate. "But I wish you had come with me. My room has a little balcony overlooking the river. The moon is shining, and there's romantic guitar music floating up from the lounge . . ." He let the words trail off meaningfully.

Where Brian was, guitars played and the moon shone. Where Morgan was, rain, flood and general disaster gathered. This was telling her something important, she thought, and she'd better pay attention.

A little defiantly, because Morgan was standing right there openly listening to her end of the conversation, she said, "I wish I were there, too. It does sound wonderfully romantic."

Morgan leaned over, shoved the phone aside, and kissed her square on the mouth. She sputtered indignantly.

"What's that? What did you say?" Brian asked.

Morgan just stood there grinning, eyes on her wet T-shirt, a puddle of rainwater forming around his feet. His dark hair hung in his face. His T-shirt had acquired a blotchy stain. His ragged old jogging shoes oozed water. He was wet, disheveled . . . and infuriatingly gorgeous. The wet T-shirt delineated more muscles than any man was entitled to, and the wet jeans clung to his hips with indecent sexiness. Sara purposely turned her back on him.

"I have to go now," she said hurriedly into the phone, before that gleam in Morgan's eyes translated into something more outrageous. "I'm going to take a hot shower and get dried off."

"Terrific idea," Morgan agreed when she hung up the phone. "A nice hot shower *à deux* is just what we need."

Sara didn't need to sort through her high school French to figure out what he had in mind. Crisply she said, "You may shower first. I'll take mine when you're finished. And I won't make you leave tonight. You can sleep on the sofa bed again. In the morning you can take your sleeping bag over to the laundromat, because it's too large and heavy for my dryer. But then you will have to make other living and sleeping arrangements. I suggest you get on with your life, as I intend to do with mine, and go back to wherever you came from."

"No, I don't think so." Morgan stepped out of his wet shoes and set them neatly by the door.

Sara had started down the hall to her bedroom, but she turned and looked back at him. The pleasantly polite statement had ominous implications. "You don't think what?"

"I don't think I'll be leaving."

"You can't stay here!"

"I don't see why not. You're my wife, and after tonight I'm more certain than ever that this small . . . misunderstanding between us can be worked out."

"Morgan, we do not have a 'small misunderstanding'! We may not be divorced, but we should be. And what hap-

pened tonight was merely an irrelevant, isolated incident."
Then she corrected herself. "*Nothing* happened tonight."

"As I've said before, I have no intention of forcing myself on you. And I certainly don't intend to be a burden on
you. I'll help in the house and around the store. I'll con-
tribute my share to living expenses. But I'm not leaving."

"Morgan, this is outrageous! You can't just come here
and...move in! I'll call the authorities and have you *dragged*
out!"

"Fine," he said cheerfully. He pulled the T-shirt over his
head. Wet chest hair curled in slick dark whorls against his
tanned skin. "They can find me in the shower."

Sara marched to the phone. The local police station
number was on a sticker attached to the phone for easy ac-
cess in case of emergency. This was an emergency. She
picked up the receiver and dialed the first number.

Then, her back to Morgan so he couldn't see what she was
doing, she stopped and pressed the phone to her chest.
Morgan had her trapped, just as he'd had in the bedroom
when she'd threatened to scream.

If she called the police, there would be flashing police-car
lights in her parking area. The sight of a male intruder being dragged by police out of her living quarters. Everyone
in the neighborhood would be peeking out windows and
craning over fences. And within twenty-four hours, at the
most, everyone in town, Brian and the Athertons included,
would know that it hadn't been some desperate criminal
captured at Junque and Stuffe; it was merely a leftover
husband that Sara McKenzie had neglected to mention.

It would make almost as interesting gossip as the tale of
the former mayor, who delighted local amateur theater
group audiences with his stage impersonations of little old
ladies, and then turned out to be a convicted embezzler, who
twenty years earlier had managed to walk away from a
minimum-security prison. Disguised as a little old lady.

"You're welcome to join me," Morgan called cheerfully
from down the hall, obviously not worried that his shower

was going to be interrupted by a man in uniform. "I'm still a great back-washer, although I am a little out of practice."

It appeared, Sara thought unhappily, that until she could figure out a discreet way to get rid of Morgan, she was stuck with him.

But only temporarily, she decided determinedly. The big danger was what would happen if Brian discovered on his own that Morgan was here. That would make her appear both dishonest and deceptive. Honesty alone demanded that she tell Brian, of course. But added to that was the fact that once she told Brian everything, the time bomb Morgan was holding over her would be defused. Brian would undoubtedly be upset and angry, and rightfully so, but at least everything would be out in the open. Then, if there had to be an unpleasant scene to get Morgan out, it wouldn't come as a total shock to Brian.

Then Morgan strolled back down the hallway clad in nothing but an innocent smile and a white towel draped around his pelvis. He broadcast sex appeal with more power than a 50,000 watt radio station blaring rock music. It came from his eyes and his smile and his chest and even his *toes*.

And suddenly Sara knew that discovery by Brian wasn't the only danger here. Maybe it was even an insignificant danger compared with another much more explosive one. The same danger she had felt hanging in the air when she'd been with Morgan on the beach. The danger she had recklessly ignored when she'd been in the tent with him.

The danger that if she succumbed and made love with Morgan, she would be lost. That she would be drawn back into the relationship they had shared before, a whirlwind of passion and laughter...and with the same instability and insecurity and lack of direction as a whirling spiral of wind.

Sara rushed past him to the security of her bedroom. She leaned against the closed door as breathless as if she had just escaped something chasing her. And then had the dismaying feeling that it wasn't just the sight of Morgan looking like a handsome-hunk-of-the-year poster that she was try-

ing to run away from; it was something within herself . . . and how could you escape from something that was
inside you?

Sara woke to the scent of fresh coffee perking. She
quickly got up and dressed before Morgan could pull another of his seductive breakfast-in-bed tactics. He had hotcakes cooking on her electric grill when she went out to the
kitchen. Delicious hotcakes, although she refused to comment on them. The storm, as was common with coast
storms, had passed over quickly, and sunshine and air that
mingled ocean scents with the fragrance of fresh-washed
grass spilled through the open kitchen window.

She didn't open the store until noon on Sundays. Often
she attended services at the little community church on the
hill overlooking town, but this morning she cleaned the
pickup. She crammed the defective tent into a garbage can.
Morgan dried his sleeping bag at the laundromat. Sara
wiped out the wet interior of the pickup cab, and Morgan
fixed a chain that had come loose on his bicycle when he'd
tossed it in the pickup the previous night. Morgan made
occasional conversation, but Sara, if she said anything at all,
confined her comments to a terse yes, no or uncommuni-
cative grunt.

When Anne Cassidy came to work and looked curiously
at Morgan, Sara was at a loss how to explain who he was or
why he was there.

Finally, in an introduction that fell somewhat short of the
requirements of etiquette, she simply muttered, without
further explanation, "Anne, this is Morgan. Morgan . . . Anne.''

Brian called the store late that afternoon to say he was
home and wanted to take her out for a special dinner because he had something special for her. A week ago the invitation would have delighted Sara, because it meant he had
the engagement ring, but at the moment it just felt like another arm of a maze she'd have to traverse very carefully.

"I'll pick you up at seven-thirty," Brian said.

"No, wait—" If Brian came here Morgan would almost certainly both reveal and identify himself. He hadn't said he was through hiding, but she suspected that was his intention. And he'd probably make things look even worse than they were by deliberately implying to Brian that they were sharing the same bed. "Why don't I come over to your place, and we can leave from there?"

"Sounds good to me. I'm looking forward to it." Brian's voice again rippled with that meaningful intimacy.

Sara immediately realized that he'd misinterpreted the suggestion. He thought she was saying in a discreet way that after the dinner she'd spend the night at his condo. That brought her up short for a moment, but she hurriedly dismissed the problem with the thought that she'd deal with it later. She might not even have to deal with it, she realized, after Brian heard what she had to tell him.

She didn't let Morgan know she was getting ready to go anywhere. She did her hair and makeup and dressed all within the confines of her bedroom. She worried that he might try to follow her on his bicycle...a ridiculous possibility, but she wouldn't put it past him. But luck was on her side. He tapped on her door and said he was going to run down to the store and get some eggs for the next morning's breakfast.

She waited until she heard the bang of the back door before grabbing a light evening wrap and tiptoeing cautiously to the kitchen to make certain he was gone. Her mouth felt dry, her throat tense.

This was preposterous. Sneaking around her own home as if she were a prisoner trying to escape. She stopped at the refrigerator for a quick drink of cold water from the pitcher she kept there. Then she saw it.

The label was ragged and half-missing, but there it was, the bottle of champagne. Back in her refrigerator, like some incriminating clue dogging a criminal. But she *wasn't* a criminal, she reminded herself a little desperately; she was the innocent victim in all this. She started to slam the refrigerator door, then changed her mind. Carrying the bottle at arm's length, as if it were contaminated, she marched out and chucked it on top of the old tent that had been stuffed into the garbage can. Then, both literally and figuratively, she wiped her hands of it.

She took a roundabout route to Brian's condo to be certain she didn't run into Morgan. She parked in the rear parking lot so that Morgan couldn't see the pickup if he decided to prowl around town looking for her. Brian was standing beside the convertible waiting for her when she walked around to the front of the building. He greeted her with a warm hug.

"I thought we'd drive down to Crown Rock Inn. Okay with you?"

"Lovely."

Crown Rock Inn, near the town of Cougar Beach south of Port Kesterson, was the classiest and most expensive resort and restaurant within a hundred-mile stretch of coast. She'd been there only three times, each time with Brian. It was the luxurious sort of place that made you wonder if all that stuff about money not buying happiness was perhaps a computer error.

Brian talked mostly about his morning golf game with several more people from the company considering building the shopping center. Sara made an appropriate murmur now and then, but her thoughts were focused on how to tell him her unpleasant news. Keep it light, she decided; play down the problems.

*Brian, darling, it appears there is a teensy little complication that will have to be taken care of before we get married...*

*Brian, darling, you remember that rather nice-looking guy who was in Junque and Stuffe yesterday morning? Well, it seems... ha-ha you're going to find this mix-up so amusing...*

Or perhaps drama would be more effective; play on his sympathies and let him come to her rescue.

*Brian, darling, I have something terrible to tell you. My ex-husband has just turned up with the most horrifying news. I just don't know where to turn or what to do . . .* She turned her face to the window and experimented with a beseeching expression.

In the end, however, she simply told him, straightforward and unadorned, trying neither to exaggerate nor underplay the problems and seriousness of the situation.

They were in the Crown Room where he had called ahead for reservations and ordered their dinner in advance. Candlelight flickered on the table. They had dined on stuffed salmon à la mousseline, wined on a French chardonnay and finished with a fruit concoction set aflame at their table by the waiter. The sweet, heady scent of the exotic dessert lingered in the air. The waitress served after-dinner coffee. Brian drew a black velvet box out of his pocket and set it on the table.

"I think you know what this is," he said. He had never looked more handsome. Candlelight gleamed in his eyes and turned his everyday, blond good looks to polished sophistication.

"Yes, I think I do, but first—"

Before she could stop him, he had opened the box. The ring glittered and shimmered in the candlelight. A big center diamond surrounded by a graceful double swirl of smaller side diamonds. Classy, beautiful and expensive. The kind of ring she had barely glanced at when she and Morgan were choosing rings, because it was so far out of reach of what they could afford.

"Oh, Brian, it's beautiful . . . beautiful doesn't even begin to describe it."

"May I put it on your finger now?" he asked.

"I want you to. Very much." Determinedly she turned her eyes away from the magnetic glitter of diamonds. She clenched her hands in her lap. "But first I have to tell you something. Something I wish I *didn't* have to tell you."

Before she could lose her nerve, she did it. She told him everything. About Morgan's dropping the divorce proceedings and her not knowing it, about his showing up, insisting she was his wife and refusing to leave.

Well, almost everything. She did leave out some irrelevant details about what went on inside a certain leaky tent. And a bold kiss during a phone call.

Brian just sat there with a stunned, incredulous expression.

"So I'll understand if you'd prefer to wait until we get all this straightened out, before giving me the ring." She hesitated and then added, with a lift of chin, "Or if you'd prefer not to give it to me at all."

Brian's fingers made galloping taps on the snowy tablecloth; forefinger to little finger, pause, little finger to forefinger, pause and repeat. A muscle in his jaw pulsed with rhythmic grip and release. Sara couldn't tell if he was about to explode at her or roar off to deal with Morgan. As it turned out, it was neither.

"I'm puzzled and disappointed that you failed to...finalize this matter at the proper point in time."

He spoke with a stiff, angry formality, but Sara was mildly relieved. At least he wasn't throwing things or yelling or making some embarrassing scene. But then, she should have known he'd show restraint; he was a well-bred, intelligent, civilized person.

"It is fortunate that we found out now, and not after we were married," she suggested in a hopeful tone.

"That couldn't have happened." Brian dismissed the possibility with a curt gesture of his left hand. "I'd already decided that before the wedding I'd have to show a copy of your divorce decree to my lawyer. Obviously I should have asked to see the divorce papers long before this."

Sara was a bit taken aback by this businesslike plan, but it was the sensible and proper thing to do, of course. She wouldn't be in this mess if she'd been as efficient and thorough as Brian was. "I'm sorry, Brian. I never meant to deceive you."

"Well, it's an awkward situation, but what's done is done, and there's no use crying about it." It was a phrase often used by Mr. Atherton, and Brian said it with his father's same tight-jawed expression. Then he turned brisk and efficient, the way both he and his father handled problems at the bank. "What we have to do now is figure out the best way to deal with the situation. I assume you do want a divorce?"

"Of course I do! I want to marry you. There's nothing between Morgan and me now."

Almost nothing...

She shouted down that treacherous little voice somewhere inside her. *Nothing*.

More galloping fingers as he considered possibilities. She wondered if he was going over the same ones she had considered.

"How do you think your parents are going to react to this?" she asked tentatively.

"They aren't going to know," he said without hesitation. "They'd be horrified."

"Brian, I don't see how I can keep it a secret! Morgan is right there at the house, eating meals, sleeping on the sofa in the living room, and he won't leave. I've thought about calling the police—"

"Oh, Lord, no," Brian said with an uncharacteristic fervency. "My parents aren't wild about our marriage now, and some messy scandal like that..." He let the catastrophic possibilities trail off unspoken.

"Then what do you suggest?"

"This." Brian tersely sketched a proposal that she tell everyone that she had to attend to some family emergency with her mother in Japan. She would then close the store and go to Nevada for the six weeks or so it would take to get a divorce that no one in Port Kesterson would know about.

"A Mexican divorce might be quicker, but if it's done in Reno we can be certain everything is legal and correct."

It was a workable scheme, Sara had to admit. Neat and anonymous. But she didn't like the idea of closing the store for six or seven weeks during her busiest season. And it would put Anne out of work. She explained how badly Anne, with her husband injured and unable to work, needed the job at Junque and Stuffe.

"And I doubt she'd be able to find anything else right off."

Brian made an impatient gesture with one hand. Plump, middle-aged Anne was another of the kind of people he tended not to notice.

"But perhaps I could leave the store open and Anne could run it alone for those weeks."

"Whatever." Another gesture dismissed both Anne and the store as trivial matters that Sara could deal with later.

"I'll have to check with her and see. I'm not sure she can be away from her husband all day. But perhaps, if necessary, they could stay at my place—"

This time Brian made a slight roll of eyes. He didn't want to be bothered with messy details. "Just get it arranged as soon as possible, however you have to do it. The more delays, the more complications are apt to arise."

"What about Morgan?"

"You'll be leaving in a day or two. You'll tell him you're going to Japan, the same as you tell everyone else. It sounds to me as though he just wants to sponge off you for free room and board, and when that isn't available I doubt he'll hang around waiting for you to return."

Sara wasn't so certain of that; he might even want to go to Japan with her. He'd always been fond of her mother. But she didn't comment. What she did say, with a small frown, was, "I don't see how I can just drop everything and leave in the next day or so—"

"What if your mother really was ill and needed you? You'd manage it then, wouldn't you?"

"Yes, of course, but—"

"Then do it."

Sara struggled to match that decisive and efficient attitude, but she kept getting tangled up in complications. "But until I go, even if it's just in a couple of days, Morgan is still going to be right there in my house." She gave Brian a sideways glance. "Doesn't that...bother you?"

"Of course it does. But you've assured me that there's no longer anything between you and Morgan, and I trust you."

A wonderfully mature and generous attitude. Sara admired and appreciated it. And felt angry and guilty with herself because deep down some perverse part of her irresponsibly wished Brian would simply storm over to the house and physically confront Morgan instead of sitting here being so calm and civilized about everything.

"Just don't get excited and do something rash such as calling the police or making some other big scene that will draw attention," he warned. "My parents have important guests from Connecticut and Virginia visiting. We must keep up appearances and not let the situation deteriorate into something...messy."

"Yes, of course," Sara murmured. She eyed the black velvet box. "Under the circumstances, I imagine it would be better if we wait until later for the ring."

"Oh, no, I want you to start wearing it right away. We've made the engagement announcement, and my parents know I bought the ring. If you're not wearing it, they'll wonder why."

"But I am...unfortunately...still married to Morgan, and wearing an engagement ring at the same time..." Sara's voice trailed off as she found it difficult to express the small sense of queasiness this situation gave her.

"Sara, it will look *peculiar* if you're not wearing the ring." Brian removed the ring from its bed of white satin and reached for her left hand. "But I can't put it on your finger if you're going to keep your hand clenched in a fist."

"Oh—I'm sorry!" Sara obediently spread and stiffened her fingers, and he slipped the glittering ring on her finger. "It's beautiful, Brian. Thank you so much."

They drove back to Port Kesterson in what Sara told herself was a companionable silence, although it felt more like the cool aftermath of a session on war strategy. Brian thawed, however, when they reached the parking lot at the condo.

His hand cupped her chin. "Come upstairs with me," he whispered softly. "We'll put some romantic music on the stereo, open a bottle of wine..." He kissed her temptingly on the corner of the mouth.

"Brian, I hate...I really *hate* to keep bringing up the problem of Morgan...but he has this terribly possessive attitude about still being married to me. If I don't come home, he may come storming over here and make some flamboyant scene that will draw attention."

"I see. Well, we don't want that." The caress on her throat and chin ended. "Very well, I suppose you'd better go home then."

Sara was uncertain if she was relieved or disappointed. One part of her wished he'd just growled, "To hell with Morgan," swept her up in his arms and carried her up to the condo. The more sensible part of her, of course, was relieved that he'd acted with judicious restraint. He didn't let reckless impulses or desires of the moment interfere with more important long-range plans.

He walked her to her pickup and kissed her good-night. She said she'd call him at the bank as soon as she'd talked to Anne about temporarily taking over the store.

Then she reluctantly drove home to face Morgan. The ring felt as brilliant as a captured shooting star on her left hand. And heavy as a chunk of lead.

## Chapter Six

Morgan noticed the ring the moment she walked in the door. He picked up her hand and inspected the glorious diamond.

"Very impressive," he commented, "if you don't mind lugging around a stone that's big enough to qualify as a lethal weapon."

"I think I can manage."

Morgan sighed as he dropped her hand. "Sorry about the cheap shot. It's gorgeous, of course. Brian has better taste in rings than he does in perfume. And his taste in women, of course, is impeccable." His expression turned pensive. "What happened to your old wedding ring?"

"I suppose I still have it...somewhere." Sara deliberately shrugged to give the impression that the ring wasn't important enough for her to be concerned about its whereabouts. Actually, she knew exactly where the ring was. Out of some foolish sentimentality, she'd sealed it in an envelope and stuck it in the bottom of her lingerie drawer.

"One of the things I've always regretted is that I lost mine. I wasn't wearing it for a few days there because I'd cut my hand on a stovepipe when I had that job with the chimney sweeper, and I never could find it again. Which, I suppose, is what comes of being, as you pointed out, disorganized and irresponsible."

She impulsively started to contradict those harsh judgments of himself, at least in regard to this matter, but stopped. There was no point in rummaging around in the past. Let the ring remain "lost." She wasn't about to bring up memories best forgotten.

"Coffee?" Morgan offered, gesturing toward the coffeemaker where he had a fresh pot brewing.

"No, thank you. I'm going to bed."

"While you were out wining and dining and acquiring diamonds, I had a sandwich down at the café. The waitress said her daughter occasionally does housecleaning for the Athertons."

"Which no doubt means you've been listening to more gossip and hearsay evidence to indict Brian and his parents for the awful crime of having money and being thrifty with it. I suppose you heard that ridiculous story about Mrs. Atherton trying to get their gardener to accept part of his pay in kitchen leftovers."

Morgan's eyebrows lifted. "Well, no, I didn't. But isn't that fascinating? And character-revealing."

"It was just malicious gossip." Certainly not something she'd checked out with Brian. Sara mentally kicked herself for bringing it up now. "Good night," she added firmly to put an end to the conversation.

"Actually, what I heard had more to do with some heated arguments between Brian and his father. The rebel in a banker's suit, fighting to get out from under his father's thumb," Morgan mused thoughtfully. "Although he's really only a temporary rebel. Deep down, he's exactly like his father."

Morgan was doing it again, Sara thought. Studying people, dissecting them, researching them. Back when they were married he was always scribbling down little character sketches and bits of dialogue, although, of course, he never had the self-discipline to sit down at the typewriter and actually fit them into a story.

"You're wrong," she said. "Brian is nothing like his parents."

"You don't think so now, but someday you'll find out I'm right. And what happens then, if you're married to him?"

"No doubt you'll be delighted to show up and say, 'I told you so.' Except that you are *wrong,* so the opportunity won't arise."

Morgan ignored her argument. "Brian has all these ambivalent feelings. Wanting to be his own man, run his own life, take over the bank and run it his own way. But at this point he can't do that. His father is in control. So he rebels in little ways, things he can control. The car. That flashy red convertible appalls his parents, of course. But eventually, he'll turn it in for something quietly expensive, like his parents' Mercedes."

She didn't ask how he knew what kind of car the Athertons drove. After all his snooping he probably knew how many pairs of socks Mr. Atherton owned. "So? I personally find absolutely nothing wrong with the idea of owning a luxury car."

"Doesn't it ever occur to you that perhaps *you* are another of Brian's rebellions? That he subconsciously chose you for the very reason that you are not his parents' vision of the ideal wife?"

"That is ridiculous!" Sara gasped, appalled at the suggestion.

"And how happy are either of you going to be when he eventually turns into a man just like his father . . . and you don't turn into a woman just like his mother?"

"Morgan, you have the . . . the wildest imagination. The most *preposterous* ideas—"

"My gosh, I'm forgetting something! How could I have forgotten this, of all things? How did Brian react when you told him that we were still married, and I'm here? Or didn't you tell him?"

"Of course I told him. He reacted like the perfect gentleman that he is. You see the ring, don't you?" She stuck her hand practically under his nose and wiggled her finger to throw the glitter into his eyes.

"He doesn't even care that we're living together?"

"You may be staying here temporarily, but we are certainly not, in the generally accepted meaning of the phrase, 'living together.' As Brian very well knows. He trusts me." She didn't mention Brian's concerns about wanting to avoid scandal with an unpleasant public scene.

Again Sara said a cool good-night and swept down the hallway

Her sleep was not particularly serene, however. She had a running series of ridiculous dreams. She and Brian hosting a barbecue at which he was wearing a tux and she a tiara. Herself with hands horrendously swollen like sausage-shaped balloons, a reaction that doctors determined was an unfortunate allergy to oversized diamonds. Driving around in an enormous, battleship-sized car with Mr. Atherton, and then realizing it wasn't Mr. Atherton at all; it was Brian.

In the morning, while Morgan was helping a customer carry out a heavy chair, Sara got Anne off alone and told her she was going to have to be gone for several weeks to take care of her sick mother in Japan. She felt self-conscious spinning the phony story, but she reminded herself that she wasn't doing it to harm anyone.

"Would you be interested in running the store alone while I'm away? It would mean considerably more money than you're making now, of course."

"Sara, I'm really sorry to hear your mother is ill. But the extra money would be a godsend for us. I'd be delighted to do it. Your ring is lovely," Anne added. "It's too bad you and Brian have to be separated so soon after getting engaged."

Sara just nodded absentmindedly. There was so much to do. Packing, writing up a list of instructions about the store, making arrangements so Anne could handle the banking and pay bills. How would she get to Reno? If she flew she'd be stuck there without transportation for six weeks. But would the old pickup make it to Nevada? She should at least have the oil changed and the spare tire fixed.

She was turning over in her mind how she was going to tell Morgan this fiction about her mother's health when he stuck his head in the door and said if she didn't need him anymore now that he'd see her later. A moment later he pedaled past the front window. She momentarily wondered where he was going. Probably to do more snooping, she decided in exasperation.

She went back to her living quarters, so Anne couldn't overhear the conversation, and called Brian. She told him that she'd arranged for Anne to take over the store, and she planned to leave in two days.

"Great, hon, I'm glad to hear it. But something has come up." He explained that he'd been discussing an important business possibility with his parents' houseguests. If everything went right, he might be taking over the management of a bank in Connecticut.

"You mean you'd move there?"

"*We'd* move there. It's important that you meet these people. I want to assure them that my new wife will fit in and be an asset to both me and the bank."

Sara didn't necessarily object to the possibility of the move, and she saw wonderful possibilities for Brian in it, but her head buzzed with all the changes it would mean. Moving across the country, a totally different life-style, selling Junque and Stuffe.

"The problem is, however, that there won't be an opportunity for you to meet them properly until this weekend." He explained about the men going salmon fishing on a charter boat, and his mother and the wives going over to the Shakespearean Theater in Ashland to see a couple of plays. But his parents had a big dinner planned for Saturday night and a more intimate brunch for Sunday morning. "So I want you to put off leaving for Reno until next week. It's extremely important that you and the Wycoffs and Chandlers meet. I won't go so far as to say that whether or not I get the position in Connecticut depends on their impression of you, but if it comes down to a decision between me and another equally qualified candidate, the wife could be the deciding factor."

The weight of the responsibility that rested on her momentarily intimidated Sara, but she quickly reminded herself she could do it. She would *dazzle* these people with her social acceptability and competence and charm. But there was still the same ugly problem that clung to her the way chicken pox had when she was a kid.

"I hate to keep bringing up Morgan, but with a week's delay it's going to start getting around that there's a strange man claiming to be my husband living in my house. Your parents may get wind of it."

"Yes, I've thought of that, and I've come up with a plan. Now, why is Morgan here?" Brian spoke a little like a teacher leading a child through a complicated problem, but she went along with it.

"Apparently he had some outrageous idea that we're going to get back together."

"Right. So if you let him think that may be possible, he'll go along with something he might otherwise flatly reject."

"I'm not sure I know what you're getting at. I doubt there's anything I could say to Morgan that will make him leave peacefully, even for a week."

"He won't have to leave."

That comment was enough to make Sara blink, but the full outline of Brian's plan made her mouth sag open.

His plan was that she would temporarily put the story of a sick mother in Japan on hold. Instead she would tell Morgan that she was definitely considering reconciling with him, but she was in a terrible state of confusion at the moment and needed time to think. And she couldn't possibly choose him over Brian if he caused a lot of trouble and embarrassment by going around telling everyone he was her husband.

"He isn't going to *hide* for a week while I pretend to think," she protested.

"No. He'll merely tell everyone that he's your brother. Brother Morgan McKenzie innocently visiting his sister for a few days."

The whole idea sounded so preposterous that Sara didn't know what to say. She saw all kinds of holes in the plan, the basic one being that Morgan would laugh in her face when she told him. Double over and howl in glee and fall on the floor laughing. Yet at the moment she couldn't come up with any better suggestion.

"Just try it," Brian said. "If it doesn't work we'll have to figure out something else."

Sara went out and told Anne that her mother's health had improved and she wouldn't be leaving for another week. Then she wrestled with this other crazy idea of getting Morgan to pretend he was her brother. No matter how she practiced saying it, lightly, dramatically, pleadingly, her vision of Morgan's reaction was always the same: huge guffaws of laughter. And she couldn't get over a certain feeling of...what? disappointment? dismay?...that Brian was so willing to let Morgan remain in her house. Shouldn't he be ranting and raving and throwing the scoundrel out? Because, even if Morgan agreed to this, and she figured there was about as much chance of that as there was of Mrs. Atherton throwing a champagne brunch for the homeless, he wouldn't necessarily play the brother act in private. Morgan's attitude toward her was definitely not brotherly.

Then she scolded herself for that attitude. She should be congratulating herself that in Brian she had chosen a man who was big enough, mature enough, not to throw foolish tantrums of jealousy. And perhaps she should work on her own maturity.

She had closed the store and was preparing dinner before Morgan showed up again. Reluctantly curious, she asked, "Where have you been all day?"

"Here and there."

"Doing this and that?"

He nodded cheerfully. He set some money on the table. "To help with household expenses."

She eyed the money warily. There was quite a lot of it. She could see a fifty among the smaller bills. "Where did you get it?"

"Well, you see, I wrote this marvelous book, and as soon as the people at the publishing house read it they started sending me money by the barrelfuls...or would that be barrelsful? Maybe I should just call it tubs of money."

"Maybe you should just tell me where you really got the money."

He managed an injured expression at her lack of faith. "Maybe I got a job as a male stripper shimmying around in bikini underwear." He put his hands over his head and flashed her a wicked grin as he did a spectacular bump and grind. "Perhaps you'd like to see the stripped-down version?" he inquired.

Sara looked the other way. She turned down the heat on the burner of the kitchen range. It was getting awfully warm in here. "Not in staid little Port Kesterson you didn't get any male-stripper job," she stated finally.

She dismissed the question of where he'd gotten the money since he obviously didn't intend to tell her. There was a far more important hurdle to surmount. She busily stirred the spaghetti sauce so she wouldn't have to look at him while she talked.

"I have been giving the possibility of our getting back together serious consideration," she said carefully.

He stopped in mid-grind and lowered his hands. "You have?"

"Yes, but your showing up here came as such a surprise... and with the complication of Brian... and everything...I'm feeling very confused and need time to think."

"I can understand that."

"And then I've just learned that my mother may be ill in Japan, or maybe she's going to be ill..." No, no, wrong story. That didn't belong here. That was next week's story. She *was* getting all confused. She swallowed and tried again. "What I'm trying to say is, I can't think straight when I'm afraid you're going to make some big uproar and scandal about being my husband, when everyone thinks I'm engaged to Brian... so what I'm wondering... what I'm *asking*," she corrected, "is that for a little while you pretend you're my brother here visiting me."

"Your brother?" He sounded as incredulous as if she'd just asked him to be best man at the wedding. He practically choked over the word as he repeated it. *"Brother?"*

She peeked at him out of the corner of her eye and saw the inevitable smile starting to form. She groaned to herself. Why shouldn't he laugh? The idea was totally outrageous. But, to her surprise, the smile didn't escalate into the expected belly laugh. Instead he removed her hands from the stirring spoon and turned her to face him.

"Look at me," he commanded.

Reluctantly she raised her eyes to his. He wasn't smiling.

"You really are considering our getting back together? And my temporarily pretending to be your brother will help you make up your mind? Maybe in my favor?"

"Yes."

She hated this, she realized suddenly. Whatever hardships and problems she and Morgan had encountered, they'd always been honest with each other, and she didn't like being dishonest now. Although she had the wild feeling, with his eyes holding hers like double magnets and the heat of his sexy dance burning through his hands to her shoulders, that she wasn't totally certain what was truth and what wasn't.

"Very well, then, for the time being I'll be your loving older brother come to pay a family visit."

"You will?" Sara looked at him in wary disbelief. The possibility that he might actually agree to the wild idea had never really registered with her. She'd been planning to call Brian back and say they were just going to have to come out with the truth to everyone about everything, hold up their heads and take the consequences.

"So, sister Sara, would you like me to fix some garlic bread to go with that spaghetti? Oh, by the way, sister dear, I put our bottle of champagne back in the fridge. I rescued it from the garbage where you must have thrown it by mistake."

Sara opened the refrigerator door. Yes, there was the same old bottle of champagne tucked way back in the corner so she couldn't possibly throw it out by "mistake" again. She was beginning to feel as if it were attached to her by some supernatural force. Had anyone ever been haunted by a bottle of champagne?

But she wasn't going to make any fuss about that minor matter now. Morgan had agreed to this unlikely proposition, but she still had enough qualms that she made him put it in the form of a promise.

"Do you solemnly swear that for at least the next week you will pretend to be my brother to *everyone,* that you will not act like a husband, not identify yourself as a husband and not cause any embarrassing scenes?"

"As surely as I am Morgan McKenzie, husband of Sara McKenzie, I do so solemnly swear," he agreed.

Sara looked at him doubtfully. He'd just sworn, as surely as he was her husband, not to act like a husband or reveal that he was her husband. There seemed a certain contradiction in terms there. Then he laughed and kissed her on the cheek.

"Honest, Sara, I won't tell. So, let the games begin! I guess this does mean we can at least be seen together in public now, doesn't it?"

"I suppose so," she agreed reluctantly.

"So how about taking your brother for a nice walk along the beach after dinner, and then he'll buy you an ice-cream cone on the way home?"

"I don't think so. Brian will probably come over or call."

But Brian neither called nor appeared. Sara, thinking there was no point in abandoning her usual walk along the beach just because Morgan *was* there, decided to go ahead with it. If Morgan wanted to tag along, that was up to him.

Oddly enough, the little farce relaxed some of the tension between them. Sara was no longer nervous about someone seeing him and speculating about his relationship to her, no longer uneasy about what sort of incriminating statements he might make to someone they happened to meet. They ran into a couple of people on their way to the beach, a woman who worked at the bank and a man who wrote high school sports stories for the little local paper, and both times Sara introduced Morgan as her brother.

The woman even said, "I can see the family resemblance," which made them both struggle to keep from laughing.

They jogged on the beach, gathered a handful of tiny amber-red agates, and watched the sun go down at the end of a shimmering golden path across the sea. They stopped at the Sea Gull Ice-Cream Shoppe on the way back.

"Black walnut still your favorite?" Morgan asked.

Sara nodded. He was just handing her the cone when the blond bookends walked in. Sara caught the oddest expression on Morgan's face, as if he were frantically trying to think of some place to hide, but it was too late; they'd already spotted him. So what was going on here?

Then, with a show of jaunty confidence, he called them by name. "Cindy! Sandy! Nice to see you again. And I don't think you've met my sister, Sara McKenzie, have you? Sara, Cindy and Sandy Simonson."

Hey, wait a minute, Sara thought indignantly, as the twins encircled Morgan like leggy parentheses. *Sister?*

But, of course, if he was her brother, she was his sister. So all she could do was watch while they fussed over him as if he were some reigning rock star.

To keep from saying something totally out of line and inappropriate, Sara marched over to the counter and busied herself wrapping the dripping cone in a napkin. When she returned to the round table the blondes were leaving.

"See you at the campground," one of them called gaily to Morgan.

Morgan gave them visual, if not literal pats on the bottom as they pranced out to their bicycles.

"What are these, reserve forces in case things don't work out with you and me?" Sara snapped.

"Never hurts to be prepared," he said blandly. "They were *very* relieved to hear you were my sister."

"What was all that about seeing you at the campground?"

"They're college students with part-time summer jobs at the campground. They live in a little trailer there. Jealous?" he added archly.

"Don't be ridiculous." For a moment there she'd almost misplaced the fact that this possibility of her and Morgan getting back together again was just a pretense.

She took a big bite of ice cream and chomped on it as if it were leather shoestrings.

The next evening Sara and Brian went out for an early dinner. Sara was dreading the first face-to-face meeting between Brian and Morgan, but it didn't happen. Morgan, after helping repair a sagging shelf in the store that morn-

ing, had disappeared and hadn't yet returned when Brian
picked her up for dinner.

They ate at a local seafood restaurant. Brian was excited
about the possibilities of the Connecticut job, and Sara realized Morgan was right about one thing. Brian really resented being under his father's control at the bank. It had
always been obvious, she realized, but she just hadn't zeroed in on it the way Morgan immediately had.

Other than asking if Morgan was keeping up the pretense
of being her brother, Brian had no comment about her not-
yet-ex-husband. He told her what he wanted her to wear for
both the Saturday evening dinner and Sunday brunch. He
wanted the guests to see her as stylish but conservative.

Except for Morgan's usage of that cloying "Sister Sara"
term that grated her nerves, things skated along smoothly
for the next two days. Sara got the oil changed and the spare
tire for the pickup repaired. She found a home for the stray
cat, because she wouldn't be around to feed it for several
weeks while she was in Reno. The Athertons announced
Brian's engagement to her in the local newspaper. Morgan
fixed some leaky faucets for her across-the-back-fence
neighbor, and the elderly woman raved to Sara about what
a marvelously handsome and helpful brother she had.
Morgan, after helping around the store briefly every morning, always disappeared and didn't return until evening. He
and Brian, whether by accident or design, missed meeting
face-to-face.

Sara began to think the whole odd, devious plan might
actually work. She was pleased, of course, yet her feelings
were unsettled and ambivalent. She didn't like the deceit. It
made her feel as if she were walking through something
squishy and slimy that dragged at her feet. The fact that
Brian, for the sake of appearances, was so willing to let
Morgan remain in her home still bothered her. For some
perverse reason she was even disappointed in Morgan for
falling for the whole phony story; he should have been able
to see right through it.

On Saturday morning a man came into the store and said he had two bedrooms of furniture from an old house he'd bought. He'd planned to hold a garage sale to get rid of it the following week, but the movers were arriving ahead of time with his good furniture from California and he needed to dispose of the old stuff immediately. He'd make her a really good deal on it, he said, if she would get it all out of the house immediately.

Sara hesitated. Building up her stock now wasn't necessarily the wise thing to do, given the possibility of a move to Connecticut. But she hated to pass up a bargain.

"I can look at the furniture now," Sara said. Anne had already arrived and could take care of the store. "But I'll have to check and see if the man I hire for heavy work is available to help move it today."

Morgan, who hadn't yet left for whatever mysterious place it was he went every day, volunteered to stick around and help. Sara, determined not to be indebted to him, said she'd pay him the same wage she would have paid the man she usually hired. Sara and Morgan got in her old pickup and followed the man to his house, which was at the end of a rough gravel road that angled off from the paved road to the expensive, ocean-view area where the Athertons lived.

Sara liked the bedroom furniture when she saw it. The price was right, and she knew she could make a good profit. She wrote out a check, and she and Morgan loaded about half of the furniture into the pickup. Morgan suggested moving the repaired spare tire from where it was lying in the back of the pickup to the carrier rack, but Sara didn't want to take the time. The sky had clouded over and rain might begin any minute, and she also needed to finish this as quickly as possible so she'd have plenty of time to get ready for the dinner at the Athertons. She and Morgan unloaded the furniture at the store and went back for the second load. It was an even larger load than the first one because at the last minute the man also decided he wanted to sell a love seat from the living room.

"I think this is the roughest road I've ever seen," Sara complained as they bounced from pothole to pothole going home. It was getting late, already past five o'clock, and she still had to wash and blow-dry her hair.

Morgan didn't comment. He was too busy balancing a couple of lamps on his knees.

But this time the rough ride didn't end when they got to the smooth paved road. The pickup lurched along like a grocery cart with a bad wheel.

Sara groaned. Flat tire? She stopped the pickup on the wide, grassy shoulder of the road, and they both got out to look. Flat tire. And the spare, as she well knew, was buried under the load of furniture.

"If you say, 'I told you so,' I will—" Sara left the muttered threat unfinished. She couldn't think of anything dire enough.

With admirable restraint, Morgan merely suggested, "Maybe we can get to the spare if we just unload that headboard and the mattress."

They unloaded headboard and queen-sized mattress but that didn't free the spare. They removed two nightstands and a bookcase, but the spare was still trapped under the love seat. In order to get everything in and avoid returning for a third load, they had fitted the various pieces of furniture together like a three-dimensional jigsaw puzzle. They had practically the whole load strewn along the side of the road before Morgan was able to drag out the spare tire. Sweat dripped between Sara's breasts and plastered her blouse to her back. A few drops of rain spattered her palm when she held out her hand.

Traffic was light on this road where most of the residents were summer or weekend people Sara didn't know. They slowed their fancy cars to stare as they drove by. Sara couldn't blame them.

Here, scattered out behind the battered pickup, the furniture that had appeared reasonably nice at the house now looked bedraggled and junky, as if they'd scrounged it from the town dump. Three mattresses flopped over the love seat, floor lamp with shade flapping in the breeze, bookcase sprawled on the ground like some sort of grotesque dead bug. Sara and Morgan's appearances probably didn't inspire confidence, either. His camouflage-material pants looked as if they'd lost a war, and her jeans had a ragged tear across the knee.

Morgan was down on his knees getting the jack in place under the pickup when a little red convertible zipped by, screeched brakes and then roared backward.

Brian stepped out and bore down on them as if he were ready to repossess their souls.

# Chapter Seven

"Sara, what the hell is going on here?" Brian demanded. His crisp slacks and sports shirt looked almost formal next to her own sweaty blouse and torn jeans.

"It's just a small mishap. I bought this furniture, and then the pickup had a flat and the spare was under the furniture..."

Which even she had to admit sounded like a rather lame excuse for standing alongside the road looking like a bag lady traveling with a collection of discarded mattresses.

"Do you realize that the Wycoffs, the Chandlers and my parents *all* saw you out here? Maureen Wycoff said it looked as if the area were being taken over by homeless squatters. Barbara Chandler thought the police should be notified that there was an encampment of suspicious-looking characters on the road. Martin Chandler said incidents such as this could seriously depreciate local property values."

The idea that her minor mishap was instantly sending property values plummeting struck Sara as a bit excessive, but all she said was, "Did your parents know who it was?"

"Of course they knew," Brian said impatiently.

"They didn't stop to offer help," Sara pointed out. Brian just looked at her as if she were out of her mind. "I take it they didn't tell the Wycoffs and Chandlers that the central figure in all this was your fiancée?"

"No, of course not. And we can only hope that they don't recognize you at dinner. If they do—" He shook his head at the possible dire consequences. "Sara, I don't see how you could do this to me! It's humiliating. I tore down here as soon as I heard them talking because somehow I just knew it had to be you."

Which was not exactly a compliment, Sara realized, but she tried to keep calm.

"I wasn't *doing* anything to you," she objected carefully. "I was simply conducting a business deal and had some bad luck with a flat tire."

Brian charged on just as if she hadn't spoken. "Sometimes it seems as if you have no sense of social position whatsoever, no dignity, no concern about appearances—"

"And sometimes," Sara shot back, "it seems as if *all* you are concerned about is appearances! You don't even care about *my* predicament here."

Brian started to interrupt but broke off as Morgan slid out from under the pickup. Smudges of grease and dirt on Morgan's face added menace to his narrow-eyed expression of hostility. In a half dozen rough strides he was face-to-face with Brian. His clenched fists hung hard and heavy as the sledgehammer standing in the tool section at Junque and Stuffe.

"Sister Sara dear, is this guy giving you a hard time?"

Morgan knew very well exactly who Brian was and that there was no need to put on the brother act here. The *Sister Sara dear* dripped with battery-acid sarcasm.

Brian took a wary step backward. "I take it this is your—" He stopped as if husband were an obscene word and changed the phrasing. "This is Morgan?" He looked at Sara as if he didn't care to speak directly to the man who had rattled his careful plans like an earthquake carelessly playing with a shelf of teacups.

Morgan didn't give Sara a chance to make polite introductions, although under the circumstances she wasn't particularly inclined to worry about etiquette anyway. Somehow she doubted the etiquette books covered the situation of introducing your not-yet-ex-husband to your future husband.

"Yes. Morgan McKenzie. And you're not going to talk to my wife the way you just did. She has more class in any one of her fingernails than you, your family, your friends and your bank have in your entire—"

"Sara's current relationship with you is nothing more than a legal entanglement created by your own incompetence," Brian cut in. He had stopped backing up and spread his feet in a challenging stance. His chin jutted out. "She is *my* fiancée."

"She is *my* wife," Morgan repeated.

Sara couldn't believe this. There they were, two hostile, stubborn men standing practically toe-to-toe, apparently ready to do physical battle alongside a public road to decide whose possession she was. As if she hadn't any say in the matter at all!

And suddenly she had had it with both of them. All the tension that had been winding inside her ever since Morgan had showed up exploded in a shower of sparks.

She shouldered her way between them and, with a palm on each solid chest, pushed. Hard. A feminine Samson bringing the male stadium down.

"I am not a possession like a...a used car that the two of you can decide the ownership of. I don't *belong* to either of you! Brian, I have had it with your preoccupation with appearances. Wear the ring you say, for appearances. Let Morgan stay in the house—just so it all *looks* okay. Pretend I'm not what I am. Hide the divorce. Don't let your parents know the truth. Brian, you *are* your father. And you don't need to worry about your parents' guests recognizing me at dinner because I'm not going to be there!''

Brian blinked as Sara hammered him with the disconnected accusations. He opened his mouth to say something, but Sara just turned her back on him and launched an equally scathing attack on Morgan.

''And you, coming here and tearing up my life, trying to seduce me and practically blackmailing me with your threats of exposure, and then going along with the ridiculous idea of pretending to be my brother—''

Both men stared at her in astonishment, their opposing claims of ownership apparently forgotten for the moment as Sara raged on.

''*You* can have your ring back.'' Sara jerked the ring off her finger, grabbed Brian's hand and slammed the ring into his palm. Then she turned to Morgan again. ''And *you* can move out of my house immediately. If you don't, I *am* going to call the police and have you dragged out because I no longer care what kind of scandal and gossip it will create.''

A car passed by, its occupants staring curiously, and Brian looked around as if he'd just realized that he had become a full-blown actor in this messy tableau.

''We'll discuss this later,'' he said stiffly, ''when you've calmed down and can reconsider the situation rationally.'' He marched back to the convertible and drove off, his show of calmness belied by the scent of smoking rubber as tires squealed on pavement.

''The man does know how to make a dramatic exit, doesn't he?'' Morgan commented. Then he wiped his face with the sleeve of his shirt and turned back to the pickup. ''I hope you have a lug wrench.''

''Why?''

''Because I can't get the wheel off the pickup without it.''

Sara considered the statement. She wanted to yell that she didn't need his help; she could get along just fine without it. But that wasn't exactly true at the moment. She could probably change the flat by herself, but she could never reload the furniture alone. Further thought made her wonder why, considering all the unpleasant things she'd just said to him, Morgan didn't just stalk off down the road and leave her standing here as Brian had done.

She asked the question bluntly. "Why are you doing this?"

"Because I love you madly, always have and always will." He sighed as though he were admitting some dreadful vice and then grinned. "Besides I can't just leave you and half a houseful of furniture strung out along the road. Property values are no doubt plunging even as we speak."

Sara caught her breath at his casual declaration of love, started to laugh at his facetious remark about property values and then resolutely terminated both actions. She'd issued her decree about his leaving her house and she was sticking to it. She wasn't going to let him sidetrack her. Fixing the flat was strictly part of their one-day business deal for which she was paying him wages.

Morgan got the spare on, and they reloaded the furniture with no more conversation than a, "Shove that mattress farther to the side, will you?" and, "Lift your end of the bookcase higher."

It was close to dark by the time they got everything unloaded and crowded into the store. The Athertons and their guests would be gathering for dinner about now, and Sara briefly wondered what kind of story Brian would tell them to explain her absence. Something creative, no doubt. Perhaps he should have been the writer.

She briskly figured how much she owed Morgan for the day's work and handed him the cash.

"What's this?" he asked.

She explained how she'd figured his day's earnings. He scowled as if he'd forgotten there was payment involved, but he finally pocketed the money.

"And I meant what I said, Morgan. You *are* leaving. There's just one thing I want to know."

"What's that?"

"Why did you go along with the crazy idea of pretending to be my brother? It was just a phony plot to buy some time until I could go to Reno for a divorce. I would have thought you had enough intelligence and imagination to see through such a devious scheme."

"Of course I could see through it." He sounded slightly offended that she had thought him so dense as not to have seen through it. "I may not be the world's most perceptive man, but you're also not the world's greatest liar. You haven't had enough experience at it. I knew this was something you and Brian had cooked up, and that you had no intention whatsoever of coming back to me at that point. But I also thought that going along with the scheme would give me a week with you, and maybe in that time you really would see the possibility of a reconciliation between us." He absentmindedly rubbed knuckles he'd scraped somewhere in the furniture-moving process. "But it appears that I was mistaken. You made a rather clean sweep with both Brian and me today."

"Yes, I believe I did."

Morgan raised an eyebrow at her pleased tone of voice but didn't comment. Instead he asked, "What if Brian comes and begs you to take the ring back?"

"I do not want Brian or his ring."

She considered that flat statement after it was said and realized that it was quite true. She'd returned the ring on angry impulse but she was over the anger now, and she had no regrets about what she'd done. She felt a little guilty that she didn't feel more brokenhearted, but everything she'd shouted at him was true. Maybe depression or sense of loss would hit her later, but at the moment she felt only a light-headed freedom and relief, as if she had just narrowly escaped entrapment in some claustrophobic place. She no longer had to try to scrunch herself into an uncomfortable mold to please Brian and his parents. She *liked* Junque and Stuffe; she didn't want some fussy antique store filled with fragile old objets d'art, a place where children were looked on as ten-fingered danger areas.

Was it possible, she wondered in dismay, that she had, as Morgan once suggested, been overly impressed with the security and wealth that life with Brian offered, so much so that she'd deceived herself into thinking she was in love with him?

"Does that mean there's just the tiniest of possibilities that you and I might get together again?" Morgan asked. When she just scowled at him, he sighed and said, "Okay, I remember. We'll get together again when the ocean turns to champagne. Right?"

"Right."

"So, I guess I'll just be going then."

"Yes, it's time you did."

"I could force you to live up to your threat and not leave until you call the police and have me tossed out," he warned. "Perhaps the publicity and scandal would be bad for business."

She was not about to be coerced or manipulated this time. "I'll write up the story for the newspaper myself, to be sure they get Junque and Stuffe and both our names spelled right," she countered sweetly.

He apparently recognized that his threats truly had lost their power. He gathered his scattered belongings. He stuffed everything in the knapsack and rolled up his sleeping bag. She wouldn't necessarily accuse him of moving in slow motion, but if he moved any slower it would take a calendar to time his speed. She got the familiar bottle of champagne out of the refrigerator and shoved it into his pack.

"Where will you go?" she asked, reluctantly curious.

"Do you really care?" he responded with mournful melodrama. He opened the door and held out one hand, his expression hopeful, but no raindrops were falling. The clouds had passed over and a full moon in a clear sky silhouetted the trees on an eastern ridge.

"I don't suppose, just for old times' sake, that you'd let me take you to dinner on our very last night together? I do have funds, you know," he added, patting the pocket that held the money she had given him.

"Morgan, you're going to need that money for...wherever you're going," Sara protested.

"Sara, darlin', I doubt that I will ever be as financially sedate and well-organized as your former fiancé. I'm never going to know exactly where every penny is. But I'm not quite as penniless and irresponsible as you seem determined to believe I am."

The sensible part of her warned that going to dinner with him was probably not a good idea...but to tell the truth, she was just a little tired of being sensible.

"Okay, I'll go. But only if I can ride double with you on your bicycle," she said recklessly.

"You've got a deal."

Sara showered and changed to a less disreputable-looking pair of jeans and a peasant blouse. When she came out of the bedroom she saw that Morgan had also showered and discarded the camouflage pants in favor of clean jeans and a navy turtleneck.

He balanced the bicycle while she climbed on the bar between seat and handlebars, something she hadn't done in many a year, and then they wobbled off down the street, Morgan humming a slightly off-key version of Bicycle Built for Two. They ate at the dark and tiny restaurant on the dock, the one where the fishermen gathered to drink beer by the mug and coffee by the gallon, and ate fresh crab that they extracted from the shell themselves. A couple of guys stopped by to talk to Morgan about fishing. As usual, he'd already made new friends with ease.

After the meal they walked down to the deserted beach. They were strolling hand in hand before Sara realized quite how it had happened.

Gentle waves rolled in out of a calm sea, whitewater breakers dancing in the moonlight. The tide was out, a thin film of water on the almost flat stretch of exposed sand gleaming like a silvery mirror. The breaking waves, so often a powerful roar, swished musically on this calm night. Sara and Morgan wound their way around towering outcroppings of rock that glittered in the moonlight as if imbedded with diamonds. On the far side of the rocks the lights of town and the dock were no longer visible, giving the beach a timeless, man-has-never-been-this-way feeling.

"You made some rather drastic decisions today. Want to talk about them?" Morgan asked.

Sara took a deep, dreamy breath of sea air. "Not particularly. What I want to do is take off my shoes."

Sara kicked off her sandals, and Morgan followed suit with his jogging shoes. When they started walking again somehow his arm was around her shoulders and hers around his waist. The sand felt grainy and damp against her bare feet. She glanced back over her shoulder and saw the trail of their footprints following them in the moonlit sand. There seemed a kind of mystical significance to the lone set of paired footprints, as if they were the only two people in the world.

"Let's build a sand castle," Morgan said suddenly.

*"Now?"* It must be getting close to midnight.

"Why not?"

Why not indeed? Sara set her sandals down and Morgan dropped his shoes beside them. Sand flew as he scooped up an impressive mound and flattened it into several levels with the edge of a piece of sea-battered plywood. Sara, using a discarded cup as a mold, added walls and turrets and towers. Morgan paved the topmost room with flat rocks and scalloped the walls with shells.

They were always colliding, laughing as they backed into each other or bumped arms or tangled legs as they reached across the fanciful structure.

"You have sand on your backside," Morgan said once, reaching over to brush her off.

Sara giggled. She felt giddy with moonlight and freedom. She could do anything she wanted now, no longer bound by Brian's or the Athertons' pinched views. "What can you expect," she asked airily, "from a woman who has no dignity whatsoever?"

"Dignity, like beauty, is in the eye of the beholder," Morgan asserted grandly.

He surrounded the castle with a moat, she topped the highest tower with a seaweed flag, and then they sat back to admire their work.

Sara tilted her head. "It's beautiful, but it looks so empty and lonely. Where are the people?"

Morgan dug in his jeans for a pocketknife and with a few deft strokes transformed some bits of driftwood into little people. He crowned the head of one with a pointed white shell.

"That's the beautiful princess who lives all alone in the castle." Morgan placed the little wooden figure in the topmost room of the castle. "She's kept prisoner there by the dastardly Duke of Diamonds." He planted another stick figure to guard the castle entrance. Sara didn't need diagrams to know who these figures represented in real life.

"I presume there's a knight in shining armor around somewhere?" she inquired.

"Of course." Morgan galloped a larger figure up to the castle entrance and after a miniature battle the dastardly Duke of Diamonds was vanquished. "And now the knight claims the fair princess as his own true love, and they live happily ever after."

Sara tilted her head. "It's not exactly bestseller material—"

"I could add some spicy details about the princess and the knight." He pushed her back against the pillow of his arm, and a fingertip brushed the soft hollow beneath her jaw. "Or, better yet, show you..."

The sand felt damp beneath her but a shimmering warmth followed his hand as it slipped under her blouse and caressed her skin.

"Remember the time we rented the rowboat and made love in the middle of a lake..." His lips whispered kisses between the words, feathery touches on eyebrows and tip of nose and corner of mouth.

Sara couldn't remember what lake it was or what state it was in, but she remembered lap of waves against the sides of the boat, feel of sunshine on her face and body, sweet magic of loving and being loved. So many unlikely places they'd made love, she thought dreamily. Capturing the moment before it escaped them, savoring both the physical and emotional bonds that bound them together as friends and lovers and playmates.

"And while we were... busy, we floated in to shore and barely got dressed before a man came along and asked how the fishing was." Sara laughed softly.

Morgan dipped his mouth to hers, one leg flung across hers as if he thought that even though she momentarily lay pliantly in his arms she might suddenly try to escape. She drifted with the kiss, feeling the throb of the pulse in her throat, the feeling of security with Morgan's arm cradling her.

Yet a sudden moment of panic made her stiffen. She shouldn't be here, shouldn't be doing this. She should escape, escape before moonlight madness... or was it Morgan madness?...swept her so deeply into a maze of tangled memories and desire that she couldn't find her way out. She twisted and squirmed, but the arm cradling her shoulders tightened like a muscular vise and the powerful leg clamped her legs to the sand.

Yet even as he used raw male force to hold her captive, his kiss was sweetly tender, his lips soft against hers. His tongue slipped between her parted lips in sensuous invitation rather than rough invasion. His hand found her breast and caged it with a velvet strength.

Her hand crept up to encircle his neck, fingertips creeping into hair that, just as she remembered, felt softer than it looked. She returned the kiss, feeling the rise of long-ignored needs, needs that hadn't been all that difficult to ignore until she was in his arms.

Thoughts swirled in the back of her head. Sensible thoughts, logical thoughts, warning thoughts. If she made love with him just once she'd lose all sense of good judgment; she'd thrust all the problems of life with Morgan into some dark corner of her mind and start rationalizing the wild temptation to go back to him.

She must not do that. She must be strong and sensible and logical...

But sensible thoughts were weak and dreary little things compared with the sweet fire of the messages from her senses. The whispers in her ear, lips brushing the fragile curve, the words indistinct but the messages of love and desire clear. The feel of his hair and skin and muscles against her fingertips, the touch tangled with the internal messages coming from her own skin and muscles as his hands caressed her. Fresh-washed scent of his hair and taste of his skin as she nibbled his earlobe. All of these combined to weaken her inhibitions.

"You always did have the most irresistible earlobes," she whispered. She bit a little harder and felt a shiver of desire course through him.

"Is that all you find irresistible?" he asked. His body slid over hers, his lean length pinning her to the sand in tempting intimacy. "I find everything about you irresistible, just as I always have. Your hair. I like the way it smells and feels. I like to run my fingers through it and feel it blowing against my face in the wind. And your eyes, when they look up at me like that, full of promise and desire..." His lips touched the curve of her eyelashes with exquisite delicacy.

She wanted to deny that her eyes held promise or desire, but she couldn't. She wanted to deny she found all of him irresistible, but she couldn't.

"I love the feel of your skin and the taste of your mouth—"

Suddenly, without warning, he scrambled to his feet, snatched her up in his arms and raced up the beach with her.

"Hey, what is this?" she yelped in surprise. As a romantic gesture, this lacked his usual finesse, to say the least.

"Look."

He set her down and together they watched the foamy tip of a wave cover half the imprint their bodies had made in the sand. Half of the sand castle went, too, melting into a shapeless mass.

"The tide's coming in. I felt one wave touch my toes and knew the next one was going to get us. I know you already think disaster follows me around as if it's attached to me with a string, and I didn't want tonight to wind up like our wet night in the tent at the campground."

"I'm impressed," Sara murmured. "It has occurred to me that you seem to have a propensity for water catastrophes."

"But all that is in the past," Morgan proclaimed. "See how I've changed and matured? How impressively I peer into the future and avoid disaster now? You might even say I saved your life. We might have been swept out to sea if I hadn't carried you to safety."

"I appreciate that. I really do. Although there is one small detail you're overlooking in this marvelous dramatization of the new and improved Morgan McKenzie."

"What's that?"

"We're shoeless."

They spotted the shoes sloshing around in the surf. Morgan dashed after them, but the waves, almost as if they were deliberately teasing him, kept the shoes just out of reach. A wave would temptingly drop one shoe on the sand but before Morgan could grab it another wave would snatch it away. Sara chased after a sandal and got doused to the knees. When the moon slipped behind a bank of clouds drifting in from the west and they could no longer distinguish the shoes from bits of floating driftwood, they finally gave up. Sara knew that the shoes would eventually be deposited at the high-tide line by morning, but they wouldn't be worth salvaging by then.

"Sorry about your sandals," Morgan sighed as they walked back to the bicycle.

Actually, Sara reflected, she'd hated those sandals anyway. Brian had picked them out, and the style suited his mother's tiny feet much better than her own generous-sized ones. One thing had to be said for Morgan, he'd never tried to dictate how she looked or what she wore.

There were, in fact, a lot of things to be said for Morgan, she thought as they walked up the steep hill between the dock and town, Morgan pushing the bicycle. He was good-natured and honest and playful. She'd had more fun building a midnight sand castle tonight than she'd ever had at one of the Athertons' elegantly stuffy dinners. And he was the only man who'd ever made her ache with need for him, the only man with whom she'd ever wanted to soar to the stars and dance on rainbows.

But none of that changed the fact that going back to him would dump her right back into the sea of insecurity that had always surrounded him. He'd probably always regard a clock as merely a hazy indicator of time, not a specific regulator of one's activities. His nose would never get skinned from holding it too tightly to the grindstone. A steady job and money would probably never rank high on his list of priorities.

So what would be high on his list of priorities?

Her. Being with her, laughing with her, loving her. She felt a peculiar lurch inside at the thought of losing all that. Even the most magnificent castle could be lonely without a prince. And so far Morgan had shown a surprising and admirable persistence in achieving his stated goal of winning her back...

At the top of the hill they mounted the bicycle again. They cruised along the deserted main street of town with Morgan singing a lusty version of a Willy Nelson song about being on the road again and Sara striking a glamour-girl pose on the bicycle, peasant blouse pulled down to expose one shoulder and bare toes airily pointed skyward. Without taking his eyes off the road Morgan leaned over and nibbled on her bare shoulder.

Brian and the Athertons, she thought with a certain glee, would be horrified.

At the parking area beside Junque and Stuffe, Sara picked her barefoot way gingerly across the sharp gravel. She unlocked the door and flicked on the light switch in the kitchen.

But right behind her came another hand that flicked it off.

## Chapter Eight

Before Sara could do more than make a brief exclamation of protest, Morgan swept her off her feet and into the cradle of his arms. With unerring accuracy he strode along the dark hallway toward her bedroom.

"Morgan, put me down!"

His intention was obvious, and it was not to tuck her cozily into bed with a chaste kiss on the cheek. Where a few minutes earlier Sara had almost been swept along with moonlight-and-Morgan madness, she was thinking clearly again now. At least more clearly than she had been then.

"Put me down!" she repeated.

"Whatever you say."

He put her down . . . on the bed. And followed her there, his body half over hers, his lips covering her face with kisses. Sara held herself very still, willing herself not to respond to the kisses that moved from face to throat and breasts, or to the hot, tender caresses of his hands or the intimate pressure of his body.

She controlled the movements of her own body. She didn't tear her, or his, clothes off or wrap her arms around him or kiss him back. But she couldn't control the fiery wellspring of response deep inside her. It flooded through her just as it always had when she was in his arms this way, making her head feel light and her body boneless.

"Sara, why are you fighting me?" he whispered.

"I'm not doing anything," she said in a muffled voice.

He shifted his weight to the side and cupped her chin in his hand. "That's how I know you're fighting me." His tone held rueful amusement. When she neither denied nor verified his accusation he brushed his fingertips across her cheek. "Why, Sara? You do want to make love with me... don't you?"

"Yes," she said in the same muffled tone.

"Then what's wrong? You no longer have any commitment to Brian. And you're my *wife*. Or have you changed your mind about the breakup with Brian?"

"No."

It was difficult to assimilate that it was only this afternoon that she had given Brian's ring back to him. It seemed long ago. She struggled to free herself from Morgan's arms. He held her helpless for a long moment, as if he were afraid if he ever let her go he'd never get her back, but finally he released her.

Sara snapped the bedside lamp on. Morgan, as he so often did, looked rumpled and sexy and much too handsome.

It took a great deal of willpower for Sara to say, "First, you go over there." She pointed to a chair by the window.

He looked as if she had just banished him to the North Pole. "Why?"

"Because we need to talk, and I don't want you touching me when we talk because I don't think as clearly as I should when you're touching me."

His small smile held a certain satisfaction at that admission, but he slid off the bed and arranged his lean form into a position of almost formal attention on the chair, as though he were a person on the witness stand. "Very well, let's talk."

"Morgan, why did you come here?" she asked. She didn't look directly at him. He might not be touching her physically, but the tender power of his eyes alone was enough to sabotage clear thinking.

"I think I've made that plain numerous times. Because I love you. Because I want us to be husband and wife again, for always," he said without hesitation. "Our splitting up was an immature mistake, and I want to rectify it as quickly as possible."

Those were the words she needed to hear but they didn't guarantee success any more than the hopeful words of a wedding ceremony guaranteed eternal bliss.

"But you will agree that there were problems in our marriage. Lots of them."

"Yes, I'll have to agree that there were." He looked troubled, his eyes on his bare toes as if he hoped he might find some helpful revelation there. "However, I think the situation now is somewhat . . . different. I've matured. So have you. We love each other and that's what really matters, isn't it?"

Sara took a deep breath and plunged ahead. She might be sorry for this. It could be the biggest mistake she'd ever made.

"Morgan, I—I'm not really sure how I feel about you. I've spent over three years assuring myself over and over again that I didn't love you. It was the only way I could cope. I'm not sorry I broke up with Brian, but I did have my life all planned and organized until you blithely rode your bicycle back into it and *un*-planned and *un*-organized it."

"I suppose that takes some getting used to."

"Exactly—"

"I think it would be nice if we renewed our marriage vows, but I won't rush you. Patience is one of the virtues I've been cultivating during these last three years. If you'll just assure me I have a fighting chance."

"Oh, yes, you have that. But there's one stipulation while I'm considering all this."

"I have to move out?"

"That would probably be a good idea." Sara sighed. "But how can I toss a shoeless man into the streets?"

Morgan wiggled his toes and grinned cheerfully. Obviously he was not about to let her off the hook and just go. "So, what's left? I've already assured you that I won't force myself on you."

"That isn't enough. You have to promise me you won't try to do what you did tonight."

"And what was that?" Morgan was all wide-eyed, boyish innocence. "A quiet dinner, a walk on the beach, an innocent sand castle construction—"

"You know exactly what I mean. To put it in blunt words, you must promise you won't try to make love to me. You won't try to seduce me."

"I wasn't exactly trying to seduce you," Morgan protested.

"You have a better term for it?" Sara didn't give him time to answer. "If you do, whatever it is, just promise you won't *do* it."

Morgan groaned. "Sara, darlin', that's like asking a starving man to turn down the big juicy T-bone that's sitting on his plate."

"I mean it." Sara warned. "Our making love would just confuse the issue and might make us rush back into something that isn't right for either of us. If we get back together it has to be because we want it with our heads and hearts and not just our bodies. It has to be love, not lust."

Morgan groaned again. "How long do you expect me to go along with this vow of celibacy?"

"However long it takes for us to be sure."

"I'm already sure. But I remember that it once took *you* three months just to decide to cut a few inches off your hair."

Sara offered no assurances of a speedy decision. "You have to promise," she stated without compromise.

Morgan sighed. "You drive a hard bargain, lady."

"Take it or leave it."

"You know, when you get right down to it, this sounds like just another version of that pretend-you're-my-brother scheme. This isn't some other wild plot you and Brian have cooked up, is it?"

"You're procrastinating again. Take it or leave it," she repeated.

Morgan took it.

Sara didn't handle shoes in her clothing section so she couldn't help him with that problem the following morning. He pedaled off barefoot but was wearing his same old jogging shoes when he returned that evening.

"I went down to the beach this morning, and there they were. I let them dry in the sun all day, and they're not bad at all." He sounded pleased with himself as he looked down at the somewhat battered shoes. A strip of greenish seaweed still clung to one.

Sara groaned to herself. She was considering pledging the rest of her life to a man who wore shoes that had spent a night sloshing around in the surf. It was not a reassuring thought.

"I found your sandals, too, but they weren't in salvageable condition."

"Thanks anyway," Sara murmured.

Other points about Morgan also were not particularly reassuring. One was his daily disappearance. That could mean he had some sort of strange job. Or it might mean he was off doing anything from kite-flying to panhandling. He'd never actually done the latter, so far as she knew, but once he'd mentioned that it might be an interesting form of character research for his writing. She made a couple of wary passes through town in the pickup while Anne was tending the store and was relieved that she didn't see him standing on any corner.

Over dinner that same evening she casually worked the conversation around to his plans for the future. If they did decide to get back together, what then?

What she meant was, how did he intend to make a living, but what he did was take her out to look at some beautiful new homes being built south of town. She wondered why, because the houses were obviously far beyond their financial reach.

Each of the houses had a stretch of beach frontage, but the house at the far end had a particularly striking view of jumbled rocks and ragged surf. They wandered around the construction site where airy rooms, soaring roof and rock fireplace were taking shape.

"Wouldn't you love to live here?" Morgan asked. "Roaring fire in the fireplace, watching the storm waves beat against the rocks..."

Yes, it was the kind of place Sara would love to live in, secluded but not isolated, elegant but not cold and aloof. The kind of house she might actually have lived in, she thought briefly, if she'd married Brian. As if reading her mind, Morgan mentioned exactly that possibility.

Sara shook her head. "It takes more than a big house and an ocean view to make a happy marriage."

Morgan hugged her as if the statement were some jewel of wisdom that pleased him immensely. "Maybe I'll surprise you and buy the house for you," he suggested. "Kind of a back-to-the-wedding present."

Morgan, always the wild dreamer, Sara sighed to herself. Long ago they used to look at houses as a form of free entertainment, when they couldn't afford anything else, and Morgan was always saying that someday he'd buy one of them for her. Someday when he sold that bestselling book that he was always going to write. But never did.

Yet, for all the nonreassuring aspects of Morgan, there were other things about him that lit up her life. The optimistic way he looked on the bright side of things. The way he just liked to talk to her, about people and events, any and everything. The way he listened, not as if he were merely paying her a polite surface attention while his deeper thoughts concentrated on more important matters ... such as bank business. His interest in the store and its customers.

The way they laughed together, over everything and nothing. The way he was just *nice,* striking up a friendship with Anne's injured husband and mowing Mrs. Denver's lawn for her. The way he helped around the store but didn't tell her how to run it. The way he lived up to his promise not to try to unfairly influence her by trying to make love to her, even though desire often gleamed in his eyes. His honesty about a brief relationship he'd entered into out of loneliness, not love, while they were separated.

The way, when he gave her a brief good-night kiss before settling down on the living-room sofa, he always said, half teasingly, half seriously, "Now if you want anything, you just yell and I'll come running."

"Now what could I possibly want in the middle of the night?" Sara asked skeptically.

Morgan just grinned.

And he did have those incredibly irresistible earlobes ...

She'd take two steps toward making a decision to renew their marriage and then nervously retreat one.

Life had been so unstable when she and Morgan were together. All the money problems, their rootless style of life, the way they lived from day to day with blithe disregard for the future. He appeared to have a tenacious determination to get her back, which she had to admit impressed her, but a lifetime together required more than that. Happily-ever-after wasn't a stationary goal, like a medal earned; it was a process.

Brian, after a formal telephone call, came to see her one evening. Always his punctual self, he arrived at 7:55, five minutes before the appointed time of 8:00. She had asked Morgan not to cause trouble, and he hadn't, although with somewhat less than his usual cheerful attitude, pedaled off on his bicycle.

Sara let Brian in. After a few minutes of polite, awkward small talk, he asked if she had reconsidered her decision about their future together.

"I told my parents and the Wycoffs and Chandlers that we'd just had a little lovers' tiff. There's still time for you to meet them."

The same old Brian, still trying to keep up appearances. She gently told him that she had given the matter considerable thought but had not changed her mind. The exchange was polite and bloodless, as unemotional as if they were discussing an account at the bank. Then Brian spotted the man's shirt hanging over the back of the kitchen chair, and some of his control evaporated.

"Sara, you haven't gone back to—" He broke off, apparently rejecting that idea as unthinkable. "Surely you aren't even *considering* a reconciliation with Morgan!"

"I'm considering it," Sara acknowledged.

"You're making a mistake," Brian warned. "He has no job, apparently no ambition and certainly no future. I suspect, although I didn't actually *see* any of it, that he may have a certain...unscrupulous charm. And he's good-looking. But certainly you have enough intelligence, to say nothing of unpleasant past experience, to know that charm and good looks are of very little value in the long run."

"Thank you, Brian. I'll give your comments careful consideration."

She knew Brian thought he may as well have been issuing his warnings to her stray cat, which had determinedly made its way across town and come back to her, but that wasn't true. She did consider his warnings. They were very real, and she didn't pass them off as inconsequential.

She weighed those warnings and her own misgivings against the points in Morgan's favor. Time and again she weighed them. On a sunny Monday morning, about a week after their non-seduction treaty, she finally made herself stop vacillating and came to a decision.

Morgan had flaws, certainly, but everyone did. And he brought a spark and sizzle, an energy and eagerness into her life that had been missing for a long time. His curiosity and interest in everything made her see things about the town and people, and sometimes herself, that she hadn't noticed before. Morgan didn't plod through life; he raced and leaped and somersaulted through it.

If Morgan had job difficulties, the store could support them both. Not luxuriously, but adequately. They'd never live in one of those beautiful homes above the beach, but the living quarters behind the store were comfortable enough. He had already indicated his desire to put down roots here, and she believed him. They wouldn't be drifting aimlessly around the country.

But one point stood out above all else. When she finally stopped balancing and weighing all the other issues, there it was, glowing like a neon sign, putting everything else in unimportant shadows. She loved him.

Strangely enough, making the definite decision gave her the same heady feeling of relief that giving Brian's ring back had, like stepping into open sunshine from a cold, dark room. She excitedly made careful plans.

She'd tell Morgan that evening. Today, unlike the days he mysteriously disappeared, she knew where he was. He'd gone ocean scuba diving with some people he'd met.

She'd make a special dinner, the chicken and mushrooms cooked in wine that he'd always liked . . . on the rare occasions when they could afford a bottle of wine with which to make it! They'd open that now well-worn bottle of champagne that was still tucked away in the refrigerator, and she'd surprise him with her secret about the rings. And then *after* dinner... A sinfully hot anticipation tingled through her body.

And wouldn't the town gossips be working overtime when she suddenly announced that Morgan wasn't really her brother after all; he was her husband!

Sara was in the kitchen, looking for the chicken recipe, when Anne came to the door and called that someone was looking for her. Sara stopped rummaging in her disorganized recipe drawer and went back to the store.

"Two someones, actually," Anne said, tilting her head toward the figures standing by the cash register. "They asked for Morgan first."

The blond bookends, leggy and gorgeous. Should she give them the news now that Morgan was unavailable or let him break it to them himself?

"Hi," one of them said. Cindy, Sara guessed, although it was difficult to be certain. "Morgan isn't around?"

"No, he isn't. I'm not sure what time he'll be back."

"He got a phone call at the campground last evening. We thought he'd be there this morning, but when he didn't show up we thought we should come up and tell him."

Sara couldn't imagine why Morgan would get a call at the campground. He had registered there, of course, but he hadn't even spent that one night there. And who would ever know he was in the area to call him? He'd never been much on keeping in close touch with his family.

"Do you know if it's some sort of emergency?"

The twins looked at each other and apparently decided that it was all right to give information about the call to Morgan's "sister."

"It was from a woman named Alana. She didn't leave a number. She said Morgan knew it and just to have him call her as soon as possible."

Alana. Sara ran the name through a short mental list of Morgan's relatives but came up with no connections. Alana could be a family member whom she didn't know needing to contact him about some family emergency, but somehow all this seemed distinctly odd.

Sara suddenly realized that the blond bookends were as curious as she was about a call for Morgan from some unknown woman, especially now that it was obvious the name was unfamiliar to his "sister." There were, Sara thought uneasily, various disturbing possibilities.

She and Morgan had been separated for over three years. He'd mentioned one relationship. Perhaps it hadn't been as casual and unimportant as he had led her to believe. Perhaps there had been other relationships he hadn't even bothered to mention. He'd apparently been in contact with this woman since he'd come here or she wouldn't have known where to call him.

"I'll give Morgan the message as soon as I see him," she said, briskly interrupting her own and perhaps the twins' speculations.

"We left a note on his door, too, in case he goes there first," one blond twin called back over her shoulder as they headed for the door and their bicycles parked outside.

"Okay, thanks." Sara gave the twins an absentminded wave.

Hey, wait a minute, she thought suddenly as the statement got through to her. Door? Morgan had no *door*.

She dashed to the front of the store. The blondes were just putting on bicycling helmets, one in a sizzling shade of neon pink, the other in equally dazzling lime green. Both helmets had glittery reflectors front and back that shot arcs of light as they moved their heads.

"What do you mean, Morgan's door?" Sara asked.

"Why, the door to his motor home, of course." The twins looked surprised at the question.

"His motor home that is...parked at the campground," Sara said, filling in the blanks.

"Space thirty-seven." The twins now appeared confused as well as surprised because it was all too obvious that this was all news to Sara.

Sara managed a laugh. "Brothers don't tell their sisters everything, you know," she said, as if this were all just some lighthearted family joke.

But what she was grimly thinking was, *And sometimes husbands tell their wives even less.*


A flurry of customers kept Sara busy for the next couple of hours, but not busy enough to keep her mind from thundering around an endless racetrack. What was going on here?

Anne left for an hour to fix her husband's lunch. When she returned, Sara, skipping lunch herself, told Anne to take care of things until she got back.

She drove down to the dock. She couldn't find Morgan but his bicycle was parked next to a van and boat trailer. Apparently he and his friends hadn't come in from their scuba diving expedition yet.

Then, on sudden impulse, she drove out to the campground. The gate attendant told her to take the second turn to the left to find the space she was looking for.

Sara stopped her old pickup at space thirty-seven and stared in astonishment. The term "motor home" covered a wide range of possibilities, everything from the small ones that weren't much bigger than a camper mounted on a pickup up to the big luxury models.

This was a luxury model, big as a school bus, with air-conditioning units on top and a sleek burgundy-and-gray paint job. The folded note tucked under the handle of the door indicated Morgan hadn't been there recently. Sara crawled up on the front bumper and peered inside the sloping windshield.

Inside, she could see all the amenities that luxury motor homes offered: sofa, chairs, carpet and drapes in the same coordinated gray-and-burgundy color scheme; a television, VCR and built-in stereo system; the dining area and compact kitchen with microwave and refrigerator-freezer; a glimpse of a big double bed with patchwork velvet bedspread in a rear bedroom. Something else that she at first thought was another television set but decided instead must be a computer.

Sara understood none of this. Morgan surely couldn't own this. Had he borrowed it...*stolen* it? Why had he kept it a secret from her? Why was he sleeping on her uncomfortable sofabed when he could have been sleeping here?

It was here, to this motor home, she realized, that Morgan had gone to get his knapsack that night she had come to the campground. And he'd never said a word about all this even when they were half-drowned in that leaky tent.

What was going on?

By midafternoon, when Morgan still hadn't returned, Sara drove down to the dock again. By then she'd had several hours to consider various other discrepancies about Morgan that should have raised questions in her mind long before this. Morgan had said he'd hired an agency to locate her. Such agencies didn't come cheaply. How had he managed that?

His clothes. His wardrobe, if his somewhat scruffy attire could warrant being called a wardrobe, was minimal, but still, now that she thought of it, there were surely more jeans and shirts than would fit in that one little knapsack. He'd been getting refills from the motor home.

The money he'd contributed to household expenses. Where had that come from?

His daily disappearances. He must have been spending his days at the motor home. The twins had been expecting him there this morning.

The twins themselves. Morgan had nearly panicked when he and Sara had run into them at the ice-cream shop. At the time she had been suspicious of his relationship with them; now she realized that his nervousness had come from a fear that they might reveal the existence of the motor home and a whole other life that Sara knew nothing about.

Her first inclination, when she reached the dock and saw Morgan, still in a wet suit, was to rush up and demand an instant explanation of everything. Instead, she contained her impatience and took a more roundabout route. Perhaps, she realized grimly, because she wanted to see how many more lies Morgan would tell her.

Even in look-alike black wet suits, Morgan stood out in the group of divers standing around a van. Taller, more powerfully built, dark hair glistening in the sunlight.

As soon as Morgan saw her, he hurriedly separated himself from the group and walked over to give her a big hug. He had a not unpleasant oceany scent. She didn't hug him back, but he didn't take offense.

"I guess it's kind of like being hugged by a rubber tire, isn't it?" he laughed.

She just made some noncommittal noise.

"Sara, you should see it down there! The rocks, the sea life—I swear that one of those seals was playing tag with me. C'mon over and meet the guys."

He put his arm around her shoulders to lead her over to the van, but Sara held back.

"I just came down because you had a phone call. The caller wanted you to call back as soon as possible, so I thought it might be an emergency."

"A call from whom?"

"I believe her name was Alana."

Morgan was surprised enough that the flippers he was holding actually dropped out of his hand. "Alana called the store?" he finally asked like a man skirting some undersea menace.

"No, she called the campground. Your blond friends brought the message to the store, since I'm your 'sister.'"

Morgan managed a laugh as he retrieved the flippers. "I'll have to straighten them out on that small detail, won't I?"

"I think there are a *lot* of not-so-small details that need straightening out. Although I imagine the first thing you'll want to do is return this woman's phone call. The call came last evening."

He dismissed the phone call with an uninformative, "It can wait." He looked at her in a speculative way. "You went out to the campground, didn't you?" He sounded resigned, like a man who has been running but now the chase was over. He was caught.

"Yes, I did. Space thirty-seven. I've been wondering ever since if you're on some most-wanted list for motor home theft. Or if you're the kept man of a rich girlfriend named Alana. And why you've been lying to me."

"Of course I'm not being *kept* or wanted for theft." His back stiffened indignantly. "Surely you know me better than that—"

"I'm not sure I know you at all."

"And I haven't been lying to you. There are just some . . . details I haven't told you."

"Obviously. And I think it's time you do."

# *Chapter Nine*

Sara watched Morgan stride back to the van. The black wet suit made a walking silhouette of his body, emphasizing breadth of shoulders and long, clean lines of his legs. Two teenage girls watched him with admiring eyes, but Sara turned her back on him and walked over to the concrete wall that bordered the parking area.

All that honesty she'd so naively treasured, she thought bitterly as she looked down on the waves crashing on sharp rocks only a few feet below. A fine mist of spray hit her occasionally as she sat there waiting for him.

When he returned he was in his usual jeans and jogging shoes, the wet suit folded under his arm and yellow scuba tank slung over his shoulder. She'd assumed, when he said he was going scuba diving with new friends, that they were providing the diving gear. She suspected differently now.

"Yours?" she asked, indicating the equipment he set by the wall. He nodded. "Which you've been keeping at the motor home?"

He nodded again. "Everything I own is there. It's been my home. A movable home."

"An expensive movable home," she pointed out.

He sat down facing her, his legs straddling the low wall. "I guess it's time I went back and filled in a few of the details of my life that I left out."

"Please do."

He reached for her hand, but she firmly folded her arms across her chest.

"At the same time that I went back to college to earn those last few missing credits, I also finally settled down to actually write something. My first attempt was a disaster, but a literary agent thought it showed enough promise that she took me on. I spent a year and a half writing the next one. And it sold."

"It did? Morgan, that's wonderful! I'm so happy for you!" She reached to give him a quick congratulatory hug, but her pleasure in the news just as quickly turned to bewilderment and she drew back again. "So why didn't you tell me? Why act like a penniless drifter? I don't understand—" Then she did understand one thing. "The woman who called, this Alana, is your agent!" Not some romantic holdover from the time they were separated.

Morgan nodded. "I have to keep in touch with her wherever I am."

"So when did all this happen? Has the book been published? Oh, Morgan, I want to read it! What's it called?"

Sara read a lot, but mostly used books that showed up in the store. She didn't keep up on new releases or what was going on in the literary world. A situation, she decided, that as of now was going to change!

"The title is *Seeking Shawn*. It's about a man whose son is missing, his desperate journeys across the country searching for the son, and the strains the situation puts on his second marriage and their child."

"So you really did make use of all our wanderings around the country. It was research after all."

He smiled. "Backed up by a good many hours of other, more tedious forms of research. The book is supposed to be released in about two months. I've been lucky enough to get some rather flattering prepublication reviews."

"Luck had nothing to do with it," Sara declared. "It was *talent*. World-class talent."

He tilted his head. "Did you think I had talent back when we were wandering around the country trying to... live on love?"

"No, I guess I didn't," Sara had to admit honestly. "But maybe I would have if I'd had anything to judge by. You never actually *wrote* anything."

He smiled ruefully. "True. But that is one of the things that has changed about me. I'll never be a steady nine-to-five man like your banker. But, during the year and a half that I worked on the book, I learned to apply, as my agent sometimes puts it in her own inimitable way, 'butt to chair and fingers to typewriter' on a regular basis. She says all the talent in the world doesn't matter if you don't do that."

Remembering the equipment she'd seen in the motor home Sara said, "Except that now you do it on a word processor. And you've been going to the motor home every day to write."

"Right." He started to stand up. "So, now that everything is straightened out—"

"Not quite," she corrected. "Why didn't you tell me? Surely you knew I'd be happy for you. Why all this charade about being a penniless bum drifting through the country on a bicycle?"

"Actually I use the bicycle a lot. Once the motor home is parked and leveled and hooked up to utilities, I don't want to unhook everything just for a trip to the grocery store. Lots of people pull a car behind a motor home, but I find a bicycle works out great and is much less bother. Keeps me in shape, too."

"Great shape," Sara agreed with an appreciative smile. Then the smile faded as she realized he was doing the same thing he had been doing all along: telling her *some* fact but not *all* the facts. He'd detoured her question about the reason for the pretense by going into irrelevant detail about the bicycle.

Yet, when she put the question to him, she did it more teasingly than accusingly. "So why didn't you tell me all this? Perhaps one of the characters in the book is a rather...umm...unflattering version of me that you didn't want me to know about?"

"No, you're not in the book. But parts of the book might be considered R-rated. Maybe I was afraid you'd be shocked." He smiled as if he doubted the likelihood of that. Some intimate parts of their marriage might have been considered R-rated, too.

"You're procrastinating and evading the main question again."

Perhaps, she suddenly suspected from the uneasy twitch of the corner of his mouth, because he doubted she was going to like the direct truth.

"Come on, Morgan, what is it? We've always been honest with each other—" She sighed, remembering her own recent shortcomings along that line. "If we're going to make it together, we have to be honest with each other."

"Actually, if you'll think back, I did tell you."

Yes, he had, she realized. The time she'd asked where the money that he was contributing to household expenses came from. "But I thought you were kidding! The same as you were kidding about getting the male-stripper job!"

"But I did tell you, and it never even occurred to you that I might be serious. You had it in your mind that I was an irresponsible drifter who couldn't possibly change." His voice was gently reproving, but he didn't dwell on her lack of faith in him. "I don't know how much you know about the money end of writing—"

"I get the impression, motor home and all, that you're not one of that legion of starving writers holed up in frigid garrets, making soup out of boiled shoe leather."

Morgan nodded. "Alana takes a dim view of that species of writer. She doesn't want her percentage in the form of a bowl of shoe-leather soup. The money she got for me didn't set a record for an advance for a first novel, but it was a nice round, six-figure number. I thought about buying a home somewhere, but I wanted to find you so I bought the motor home instead so I could look for you. And then it finally occurred to me that I now had the money to hire someone to find you. Which I did—and so here I am."

"Which still doesn't explain why you kept it all a secret. When I think of us lying out there in that leaky tent, with the water rising around us, when we could have been in that big, comfortable motor home—!" Sara shook her head, still mystified.

Morgan stood up. He braced one foot on the wall. "Sara, I didn't tell you because I wanted us to get back together on the basis of love, not my changed financial status. I wanted the money to be a plus *after* we were back together, not the reason for it."

Sara just sat there, frozen by the shocking words. Somewhere beyond the rock jetty a warning buoy clanged melodically. A gull swooped down and strutted nearby, looking for a handout. The breeze ruffled Morgan's dark hair and swept her own into a tangle around her face. She brushed the blowing strands, damp with sea spray, out of her eyes.

"That's your real opinion of me, that I'm some sort of money-hungry gold digger who'd marry a man for his money?" The shock reverberated through her. But she shouldn't be surprised, she thought grimly. He'd come close to accusing her of exactly that with Brian.

"No, not exactly—" He squirmed as if the rock wall were an uncomfortable seat, but she suspected that wasn't all that was uncomfortable.

"Morgan, that...that's insulting! It's degrading and humiliating and—" She jumped to her feet as she searched for more scathing words but couldn't find ones that sufficiently expressed her outrage. Nice, she had thought of him earlier. *Nice!* And now this.

He reached for her. "I didn't mean it that way. I just wanted to be sure—"

She jerked away. "You were afraid that as soon as I found out you had some money that I'd come flying into your arms to grab a share of it. So you decided to run me through a little character test first."

"You're making it sound as if I did something really low-down and unscrupulous—"

"Because low-down and unscrupulous is exactly what it was! Morgan, how could you? How could you think that I was the kind of cheap, greedy person who—"

Sara broke off and ran to the pickup. She jumped in, tears mingling with the ocean spray beading on her face. She turned the ignition key. Nothing happened. She worked the gas pedal as if she were practicing some new stomping dance and pounded on the dashboard in hurt, angry frustration. One or the other action finally had some effect, and the engine grumbled to life.

She backed in a sharp arc, scrunched the gearshift into first and headed for the road leading up the hill from the dock. She, however, she realized in frustration, was not the master of the dramatic exit. The pickup groaned and wheezed as it struggled up the hill, lumbering along as if at any moment it might give a last dying gasp. She pounded on the dashboard again. She should have heeded Brian's advice to get a new pickup before this one collapsed completely. She couldn't tell if it was engine or transmission or what, but something was drastically wrong. She could walk faster than this. She could *crawl* faster than this.

In the rearview mirror, she could see Morgan gaining on her, scuba gear draped haphazardly over both him and the bicycle.

It was a race ludicrously acted out in slow motion, Morgan leaning low over the handlebars as he strained to catch her on the steep hill, the old pickup groaning in protest against the floorboarded gas pedal. There were no other vehicles on the road.

Morgan caught up with her. Sara refused to turn her head to look at him, but she could see him out of the corner of her eye.

"Sara, you're making...way...too much out of this," he yelled, grabbing for breath between words. "It isn't all that important."

"I happen to think it is *very* important!"

Sara kept both hands on the wheel and her eyes straight ahead, as if she were driving the Indy 500 instead of snailing up a hill at some five miles per hour. She pumped the gas pedal, urging more speed. Slowly, complaining noisily with every inch gained, the pickup began to pull ahead.

"Sara, sometimes I think your head is more full of *junque* than your store is!" Morgan yelled after her.

"And yours is even more full of *stuffe!*" she yelled back.

Sara reached the top of the hill just ahead of the bicycle. She still had the gas pedal to the floorboard, and the pickup, with some strange new clattering sounds and a belch of blue smoke, unexpectedly shot forward.

Sara roared toward home with tears streaming down her cheeks. She had been disturbed and confused when she'd first realized Morgan had deceived her, but now that she knew the terrible reason *why,* she ached with the hurt of betrayal. He'd proclaimed his love for her, but how much could he really love her if he didn't even trust her enough to share the truth of his success with her? And he was wrong! She'd decided before she knew anything about his money and success to go back to him.

Not that she'd ever tell him that now.

As soon as she got home she tore through the house gathering up his stuff and piling it outside the back door. She no longer needed to be concerned that she was tossing him shoeless and homeless onto the streets! He could go loll around his fancy motor home, listen to his stereo and sleep in his big double bed.

It really would be when the ocean turned to champagne before they got back together, she thought grimly.

Thinking of champagne reminded her of the well-traveled bottle still in the refrigerator, and she was adding it to the pile when he arrived on the bicycle. He disentangled himself from his scuba gear.

"There are a few things I'd like to add to our conversation," he said in a stiff tone.

Sara dangled a pair of his briefs, the bikini-style ones in black decorated with a single lightning bolt of red, over the pile. She let go and, like some risqué arrangement for an advertisement, the briefs dropped neatly over the neck of the bottle of champagne.

"I didn't come here with the deliberate intention of deceiving you. I just wanted to find you. As soon as the agency I hired got an address on you, I headed directly for Port Kesterson. But the motor home started overheating, so I stopped at Cougar Beach to have it looked at. The garage said they couldn't get it fixed until the following day, and I was so impatient to see you that I jammed some stuff in a pack and came the rest of the way on my bicycle."

"And when you got here you took one look at Junque and Stuffe and knew at once that I'd turned into some money-hungry gold digger."

"Of course not. I was impressed with what you had done on your own. I was hot and tired when I got here...it is, I believe, about a twenty-six-mile ride from Cougar Beach...and you were busy in the store so I just took a shower and crawled into bed. I thought you could take me back to get the motor home later, but when that didn't work out, I rode the bicycle back down there the next day and brought the motor home to the campground."

"So at what point did you decide I was this greedy gold digger?"

"Sara, don't put words in my mouth." Sara started to interrupt, but a dangerous glint in his eyes stopped her. "I didn't have that crude 'gold digger' opinion that you seem determined to pin on me. But several things shook me up. One was our discussion about the cause of the breakup of our marriage. You said *money* was the reason. Which certainly suggested that you thought money alone would solve our problems, and I doubt that money alone solves much of anything. I thought it vital that our getting back together be on the basis of love and a greater maturity in both of us. I didn't want the money to be an influence.''

"And deceiving me by pretending to be a homeless drifter wearing sea-soaked shoes expressed *maturity?*" Sara challenged.

"I suppose not," he sighed. "But I also found it quite meaningful that you had chosen a rich fiancé, particularly when, so far as I could determine, wealth was his main attraction."

"Then you didn't look far enough to see that he is also dynamic, ambitious, good-looking, self-confident, mature, hardworking, reliable— And he never seemed to think I was marrying him for his money!''

Morgan blinked at her listing of all Brian's nonmonetary assets. "Maybe you made a mistake giving his ring back."

"Maybe I did!''

Morgan eyed the pile of his belongings stacked outside her door and then simply stalked off and left them.

Sara turned and slammed the door so hard that the wind chimes by the kitchen window rattled. Anne came to the door of the living quarters and peered inside.

"Is something wrong?''

Something wrong? Everything was wrong. Sara felt as if her emotions had just been run through a blender and her thoughts through a malfunctioning word processor. Anger and frustration and hurt boiled with pangs of loss and bewilderment. At the moment the last thing she felt like doing was being friendly and cheerful to customers in the store.

"Could you handle things here for the rest of the afternoon?'' she asked Anne. "I—I have to see what's wrong with the pickup.''

That was true enough. But right now what she intended was to drive out to a secluded, seldom-used little cove where she sometimes went when everything seemed to be going wrong. The surf was wild there, crashing against the rocks with a fury that always seemed to put her problems in perspective. She hadn't been there recently, but she'd gone there a lot when she'd first come to Port Kesterson, still aching over Morgan. It seemed ironic that after all this time Morgan was the reason she was going there again.

She was not, however, going anywhere today, she discovered when she got in the pickup. It didn't show so much as a twitch of life no matter what she did to it. She finally trudged down to the garage that did her repair work and got the mechanic to come back with her to take a look at it.

He poked around in the engine, crawled underneath the pickup, and asked her to describe symptoms. One of which, she could see, was an ominous pool of fresh oil collecting underneath the engine.

He spared her the technical details, just gave her the bottom-line bad news. "It'll cost you a bundle more to fix than it's worth. You'd be better off just calling that auto wrecker down at Cougar Beach and see if he'll take it."

"What's it worth in this condition?"

The mechanic's answer was laconic. "If you're lucky, he'll haul it off for nothing. If you're not, you'll have to pay him to take it away."

The only thing to be said for the situation, Sara thought bleakly, was that it gave her something to think about other than Morgan.

She obviously had to have a new pickup. Just as obvious was the fact that she had no way to get around to look for one. Nor a bank account of sufficient size to buy what she needed.

The thing to do, she realized reluctantly, was go to the bank and arrange for a loan. Then she'd be in a position to bargain with cash for a new pickup. But if she went to the bank she'd inevitably run into Brian, and that she didn't want to do. He'd ask about Morgan and, when she told him things hadn't worked out, he'd somehow manage to hint, if not outright say, "I told you so."

She mulled it over until the following day. Then, because she had no delivery vehicle, she lost a sale on some of the furniture she'd purchased on that disastrous day of the flat tire. She had to do something immediately. She decided, if she timed everything right, she might be able to slip into the bank and arrange for the loan while Brian was out to lunch.

She walked down to the bank at ten minutes past one. Brian always took his lunch hour promptly at one o'clock.

Except today.

He was just coming out the side door of the bank when Sara reached it. They looked at each other warily.

Brian spoke first. "Hello, Sara." His tone was cool but civil.

"Hello, Brian." She saw his quick glance in both directions to ascertain if she was alone. The glance apparently also took in the fact that she was not carrying the blue cloth bag in which she always brought deposits to the bank, which meant she was here for some other purpose. She was surprised at the glint of interest in his eyes, as if he wondered if she had come to see him.

"Could I help you with something?" he asked.

No point keeping facts from him. He'd find out quickly enough that she'd been in asking for a loan. It was another point on which he could say, if not directly to her at least to himself, "I told you so." She briefly explained her problem with the pickup and the need for a loan.

"I've decided to take your advice and buy a new pickup rather than another used one. I thought I'd talk to Maryanne about it." She picked a name at random among the people she knew at the bank.

Brian made no comment, merely said, "Maryanne doesn't handle that type of loan. But I can take care of it."

He did, briskly and efficiently. And not once did he say "I told you so." She realized he was using his authority to put the loan through considerably faster than it would normally take, and she awkwardly thanked him. She stood to go, but he stopped her with a question.

"I assume Morgan has some means of transportation other than that bicycle to take you down to Cougar Beach or up to Coos Bay to look for a new pickup?" Port Kesterson had no new-car dealerships.

"I'll probably just look around by myself," Sara said evasively.

"But you and Morgan have decided to reconcile. I know you told him, the same day you returned my ring, that he had to move out, but I see his bicycle still parked at your place. All night," he added meaningfully.

"Things aren't always what they appear," she said without going into details. Then she decided she may as well give him the opportunity to say it. He hadn't said it on the matter of her needing the new pickup, so he must be bursting to say it now. "As a matter of fact, Morgan is out, as of yesterday. If you care to look, you'll see a pile of his belongings stacked outside my door. Things didn't...work out between us."

"I suppose, to be polite, I should say I'm sorry to hear that. But I'm not sorry. So I won't say it." He smiled slightly, as if the image of Morgan's belongings tossed into the yard pleased him.

"No 'I told you so'?"

Brian smiled again. "Would it make you feel better if I said that? Then you could feel a self-righteous anger at me for saying it. As it is, you don't know quite what to feel."

"I suppose you're right," she admitted.

"Look, you're going to need some way to get around to look for a pickup. How about if I take you on Saturday?"

"I don't think I can wait until Saturday."

He hesitated momentarily, but finally said, "Then I'll take some time off to go with you during the week."

"That's very kind of you—" To say nothing of surprising, she thought. She'd never known him to take a working day off for anything less than a one-hundred-and-two-degree fever and the flu. The new and improved Brian Atherton? "But I don't think so. Thanks anyway."

Between customers at the store, she shopped by phone the following day, calling car dealers all up and down the coast to compare prices. She got the field narrowed down, but she still didn't feel she could actually buy one of the pickups without seeing it and making a test drive.

After closing time, feeling rather like a toy robot with a rundown battery, she decided to walk down to the beach.

Usually the endless rhythm of the waves soothed her, but today she was unhappily aware of only one thing. The ocean hadn't turned to champagne...and she and Morgan weren't together.

The waves were big today, gray-green tubes crashing into white foam. She picked up a sea-polished agate, a lovely warm amber color, and absentmindedly rubbed it between her fingers as she walked.

She sat down on an old driftwood log to watch several surfers a short distance out from the beach, just beyond where the breakers started to form. Oregon's rough coastline, cold waters and often irregular waves didn't draw surfers the way California's ideal surfing beaches did, but there were a few.

Two of the surfers spent more time floundering in the whitewater than they did on their surfboards, but the other one was pretty good. He skimmed just ahead of the breaking wave, body balanced on the speeding board like a seaborne cat. Sometimes he spilled off the board at the end of the ride, but often he managed to cut back over the end of the wave and stay upright.

Sara envied them. They all seemed to be having so much fun, so happy and carefree. She used to surf a little, when she and Morgan were in California, although she'd never tried it here. Maybe she would. She tried to get excited about the prospect, but one discouraging thought intruded. She'd be doing it alone.

Finally the surfers headed for shore. They came out of the water just a few yards down the beach from Sara, laughing and talking. All three were in wet suits. Until then Sara hadn't realized that two of the surfers were women.

Blond and leggy women, she saw with an unwelcome jolt of recognition. And one was male, his dark hair and lean body all too familiar.

Morgan and the blond bookends.

# Chapter Ten

Sara's first thought was that Morgan looked anything but heartbroken. No sign of the drained emptiness that had brought her to the beach. Perhaps her first suspicion that he had a backup relationship with the twins in case things didn't work out with her had been correct.

Her second thought was that no way did she want to be caught here watching them like some wallflower who hadn't been invited to the prom. She looked around frantically for someplace to hide before they spotted her, but running for the rocks or leaping behind the driftwood log would only make her more noticeable. So she sat very still, the first time in her life that she'd ever hoped to be mistaken for a bump on a log.

No such luck, of course. Morgan spotted her first. He stopped short, then, without so much as a nod of recognition, headed up the beach toward a Volkswagen van. But one of the twins recognized her.

"Sara, hi! We didn't realize that was you sitting there. Hey, Morgan, come on back," she called after him. "Don't you know who this is? It's your sister!"

Obviously he hadn't yet straightened them out on that minor detail.

The twins set their surfboards down and came over to the log. Even wet-haired and makeup-less they looked like models on a shoot. But they were as smiling and friendly as a pair of puppies. They chattered about the spills they had taken, how invigorating the water was, how they wished they could surf as well as Morgan. Their skin glowed with pink, healthy radiance, and they didn't even seem to notice the chilly wind blowing down the beach.

Sara, who had absentmindedly left without a jacket, suddenly realized how cold she was. She felt neither pink nor radiant, and an unattractive uprising of goose bumps prickled her arms.

"Morgan, it's Sara," the other twin yelled, apparently thinking Morgan still hadn't realized it was his "sister" on the log.

Morgan reluctantly turned and came over to stand a few feet away. He jammed the surfboard upright in the sand. He looked at Sara as if he'd like to do the same to her, with her head aimed into the sand.

"We were just going to go uptown and get a hamburger for dinner. Maybe you'd like to come along?" The twin looked at Morgan, obviously expecting him to echo the invitation.

"Thanks, but I have . . . other plans," Sara said.

"You'll have to excuse our lack of enthusiasm at this unexpected meeting," Morgan said, his words directed to the twins but his eyes meeting Sara's with glitters of frost. "We have a little family feud going on."

"Oh, that's silly," the twin said. "C'mon, Sara—"

Sara stood up. "Thanks, no."

"Would you like a ride to the store, then? We're using the van today, so we could carry the surfboards, and there's plenty of room."

Sara declined again, and the trio, with two, not three friendly waves, headed for the van. Sara went back the way she had come on the beach. She sighed to herself. She wanted to dislike the twins, but it really wasn't possible.

Morgan, however, was a different story.

Sara rather expected that Morgan would take advantage of knowing she was away from home and go by in the van to pick up his belongings stacked outside her door, but when she got home the pile was still there. Including the bikini briefs gaily decorating the bottle of champagne. She gave the pile a resentful kick as she passed by.

Sara opened a can of soup for supper. She ate alone, all the time thinking about Morgan and his blond bookends having a fine time with their hamburgers. And then what would the happy trio do?

*Two* blondes would surely make for complications. But Morgan was no doubt up to the challenge.

She gave most of the soup to the cat.

The following day Brian called again to ask if she needed help looking for a pickup. This time Sara said yes.

"Tomorrow?" she suggested.

"Let's see, I have a couple of appointments... But I'll postpone them or get someone else to handle them," he said hastily, as if afraid she'd change her mind. "Tomorrow will be fine."

They settled on a time for Brian to pick her up. Sara was surprised and impressed that he didn't at the last minute find some reason he absolutely had to be at the bank and suggest putting the pickup-buying expedition off until the weekend. He was obviously going out of his way to be helpful and cooperative. And the fact that he was willing to take the day off showed how much he wanted to be with her.

*Had* she made a mistake giving his ring back?

\* \* \*

Brian kept their nine o'clock appointment by arriving at five minutes to nine. Promptness was good. A woman who shared her life with Brian would never find herself five minutes late, looking down a highway at a just-departed bus, or across a stretch of water at a just-departed ferry. Both of which had happened to Sara and Morgan.

Sara was just getting into Brian's red convertible when a bicycle wheeled into the parking area beside the store. Morgan's gaze took in the sight of her and Brian and the car as if he were noting details for an exposé.

Had he come to make apologies or amends? Sara felt an odd sort of breathlessness that she tried to keep out of her voice. "Did you want to...see me about something?" she called.

Morgan jerked a thumb toward the pile of his belongings. "I just came to pick up my stuff."

No apologies. No amends.

"Don't forget your bottle of champagne." She slammed the door of the convertible and looked the other way. When she surreptitiously glanced back as Brian turned the car around in the parking area Morgan was spreading a shirt on the ground and bundling everything into it. He tied the shirtsleeves together and jammed the Dom Perignon, label now entirely missing, on top.

For one wild moment, Sara thought about leaping out of the car and racing back and throwing herself in his arms. But Brian, as if he suspected she might be having such an irrational thought, suddenly gunned the engine and they shot out of the parking lot.

Sara decided she was grateful. He had perhaps saved her from making an impulsive mistake. She had a momentary vision of Morgan and the twins having some happy champagne party tonight.

Not that she gave a damn, she assured herself defiantly.

The best quotation Sara had gotten on the new pickup she wanted was from a dealer at Cougar Beach, so they drove down there first. The specific pickup she'd been interested in had been sold minutes earlier, however, and if she wanted that particular model and equipment they would have to order it. She couldn't get along without a pickup for that length of time.

They went to the two other dealerships in Cougar Beach, but neither had what she wanted in their new-car lineups. The salesman mentioned a used pickup that might interest her.

"Sara, you don't want something secondhand," Brian said. "There's no point in buying someone else's problems when you have the money available to buy a new vehicle. It's always better for business to look prosperous—"

But when Sara gave him a small scowl he backed off on the advice. "But it's up to you, of course."

The used pickup, although it looked good, had far too many miles on the odometer to suit Sara, and she turned it down.

They drove back up the coast to Coos Bay, passing through Port Kesterson on the way. Sara determinedly did not even look at the turnoff to the campground when they passed it, but when they went through Port Kesterson she spotted one of the twins bicycling past the grocery store. Did that suggest Morgan and the other twin were off doing something together?

Sara resolutely pushed away the hot, disturbing visions that came to mind.

In spite of all the pickups that were available in Coos Bay, Sara still couldn't find exactly what she wanted at a price she wanted to pay. Brian, although Sara could see him occasionally gritting his teeth, refrained from giving advice and was admirably silent.

But by midafternoon he finally said, "Look, why don't we go get something cold to drink while you think a little longer about that blue half-ton at the last place? It looked good to me."

"A stick shift would get better mileage than an automatic—"

Brian didn't argue the merits of stick shift vs automatic. He took her arm and propelled her lightly toward his convertible. "If you don't need something cold to drink, I do."

They found a fast-food place and carried their drinks out to a table on the covered patio. She did need a cold drink and a little relaxed time to think, Sara realized as she sipped the frosty liquid.

"You've been very patient, Brian," Sara said. "Thank you. I appreciate that. You've also been rather silent."

"Not advising you on everything from what to wear to what to eat as I've always done? Although I did slip up once, on the matter of the secondhand pickup, didn't I?" He smiled somewhat ruefully. When Sara didn't comment he said, "There is one thing I have to say."

"Oh?"

"Perhaps you don't really need a pickup at all."

"I don't understand. I can hardly run Junque and Stuffe without one."

He reached in his pocket and set a small, sparkling object on the table between them. The ring. That beautiful swirl of diamonds.

"I'm going to Connecticut. I got the job managing the bank there—"

"Brian, that's marvelous! I'm so happy for you."

"I want you to be there with me, as my wife. We'll just erase that unpleasant little scene alongside the road that day. Cancel it as if it never happened. You can get your divorce here, or go to Reno and do it, and then join me in Connecticut." He smiled. "In which case you won't be needing a pickup."

Sara studied the glittering ring Brian was offering her again. She knew that it had not been easy for him to do this, to swallow his pride and ignore all the ugly, accusing things she had shouted at him that day on the roadside. She could also see that her accusation about his being too much like his father had perhaps made an impression on him, and he had made a determined effort to be different today.

Sara leaned back in her chair and closed her eyes. Maybe, if she tried very hard, she could simply blot out these past days with Morgan. Pretend they had never happened. Chalk it up to one of those dream episodes like the ones that occasionally turned up on TV programs. Put her life back the way it was before Morgan showed up and sent everything skittering and crashing like a stray earthquake passing through.

Yet when she opened her eyes Brian saw something there that made him say quickly, "You don't have to decide right now. I just want you to think about it. I won't be leaving for a couple of weeks. Look, my folks have a pickup that the gardener uses. I'm sure you could use it for a few days while you make up your mind—"

"Thanks, but I've decided to buy that blue half-ton we just looked at."

Brian didn't try to talk her out of the decision. Obviously trying to be as cooperative as possible he said, "It could be useful in Connecticut. Maybe you'll want to start an antique store there."

An antique store. Sara doubted if Brian realized how meaningful those two words were, but she did. Brian had many good points. She'd always known that. But he would always be Brian, always have the basic Atherton viewpoint on life and the world.

They discussed whether the pickup could be bought for any less than the last price the salesman had quoted. Brian thought it could. They returned to the car lot and Sara made the cash offer Brian had suggested. After much conferring with unseen higher-ups the offer was finally accepted. Sara assumed she could simply drive the pickup home, but that turned out not to be so. They said they had to run it through the shop for a final service check. Brian stepped in then and got them to agree to deliver the pickup the following day so she wouldn't have to make another trip for it.

Sara thanked him again when they were back in the car. "You always know how to handle things."

"Does that mean I've handled our personal situation right and you'll come to Connecticut with me?"

Sara hesitated and finally said, "I'll think about it."

Sara did think about it on the drive home. She leaned her head back on the seat and closed her eyes and thought about it very hard.

Brian stopped the convertible near the door to her living quarters. "Would you like to go somewhere for dinner?" He glanced at his watch. "I could pick you up again in a couple of hours."

"No, I don't think so. Thanks anyway. But you've been a wonderful help today. Thank you."

He looked at her with the other larger and much more important question about their total relationship in his eyes. Then, with a sigh, he answered it himself.

"You're not coming to Connecticut with me. You won't marry me."

"I'm sorry, Brian. No. I can't marry you. But you know I wish you the best of everything. Wherever you go."

"Sara, I know I can sometimes be... too much like my father. But I might be able to change in some ways—"

Sara shook her head. "Maybe it's because I know *I* can't change."

"You don't have to—"

"I can't change the fact that I love Morgan," she said softly.

Which still didn't mean she and Morgan could make a go of a reconciliation, she thought to herself as she went inside. She absentmindedly bent over to pick up a sock Morgan had missed when he'd bundled his belongings together. Her acknowledging to herself that she still loved him didn't change how he had deceived her. Or why.

And yet, considering the situation from a calmer perspective than she first had, she could see parallels with her own reservations about their getting back together. She hadn't wanted to blur the issue with the physical magic they had always found together; he hadn't wanted money to affect the decision. Because deep down they were agreed on one vital point: the only thing that really mattered was love. They had to get back together on the basis of *love* or it would never work.

And they had that. Or did they? She was now sure of her love for him, but she was suddenly not so sure of Morgan's feelings for her. Perhaps their last breakup had been the final one for him. Perhaps he was no longer even interested in a reconciliation.

If she'd had the pickup, she'd drive right out to the campground and confront him. Tell him she loved him and wanted him back. She stroked the sock against her cheek, feeling in its clean softness some essence of Morgan. The thought that a stray sock was all she might ever have of him was enough to send a pang of panic through her.

So, she thought recklessly, was she going to let the small obstacle of a lack of transportation stop her? It was only some six or so miles to the campground. She had feet! She should be able to walk it in a couple of hours at the most.

She quickly changed to clothes and shoes more comfortable for walking and set out. On sudden impulse she dashed back to the house, ran to her bedroom and collected that envelope that had lain sealed and untouched at the bottom of her lingerie drawer for so long. She tucked it in the rear pocket of her jeans. Smiling to herself as she thought of Morgan's inevitable collection of mismatched socks, she stuffed the sock he had dropped into her other pocket.

The evening was pleasant, almost windless. Rays of late sunshine from the red-gold ball that appeared to hover a few inches over the sea filtered through the trees that separated highway and the dropoff to the beach below. A painted white line reserved a narrow section of pavement for bicycles, and Sara walked in that area. Traffic was light. A couple of cars stopped to offer her a ride, but the occupants were no one she knew and she declined.

The first stretch of highway out of town was level and the going easy. Sara walked rapidly, thinking about what she was going to say when she reached the motor home. She tried to hold a pleasant vision of Morgan welcoming her with open arms, but various not-so-pleasant possibilities intruded. Morgan could be involved with one or both of the blondes. He might reject her right in front of them. He might say he'd made a mistake in ever coming here.

But that was just a chance she had to take.

After the first level easy stretch, the highway broke into a series of winding dips and rises as it followed the rough coastline. Something was uncomfortably rubbing her left foot, and she had to stop and rearrange her sock. She was thirsty. The backs of her legs ached on the long upward slopes. She'd stepped in something black and sticky that had been used to patch a bad place in the road, and her right shoe made a slurpy-sucking noise with every step she took.

She envied the bicyclist whizzing down the hill toward her. Then, as the bicycle skidded to a stop just a few feet from her, Sara recognized the long blond hair hanging below the helmet that glowed like a pink sun. Although, as usual, she was uncertain whether the name that went with the pretty face was Cindy or Sandy.

"What in the world are you doing walking way out here?" the surprised twin asked.

"It's a long story," Sara said. "I suppose your sister is . . . with Morgan?"

"No, she's working this evening." This twin was looking at her so oddly that Sara glanced down to see if she was missing some essential article of clothing. The girl also appeared uncharacteristically hostile, more the snarling guard dog than the friendly puppy.

"Morgan finally told you, didn't he?" Sara asked. "That I'm not his sister, I'm his wife." That would explain the changed attitude, of course. She was a competitor for Morgan's affections now, no longer a nonthreatening sister.

"He told us." Yes, the twin definitely sounded hostile.

"So why be angry with me?" Sara flared. "Morgan is the one who deceived you and let you think he was some eligible bachelor."

No, that wasn't totally accurate, Sara admitted to herself. He'd only been playing the brother part she'd asked him to play. But he still could have let the twins know some way that he wasn't available.

"We like Morgan. We think he's a wonderful guy. He's treated *us* like sisters. And we don't like what you did to him."

"What *I* did to *him?*" Sara practically yelped. "Did he tell you what *he* did to *me?* That he didn't even tell me he was a successful writer because he thought I was some money-grabbing gold digger?"

"He mentioned that. But he also told us how he went back to tell you how sorry he was and try to make things right this morning, only to find that you'd already rushed back to your banker boyfriend." She looked at Sara's left hand as if expecting to see the ring there.

"My old pickup finally gave up and died, and when I went to the bank to arrange a loan to buy another one Brian offered to drive me around to the car lots. That's where I was going with him this morning. He suggested we might get back together, but I told him I still love Morgan. And then, because I didn't have any way to drive to the campground to tell Morgan that, I decided to walk out there. Which twin are you, anyway?" Sara demanded. She had just revealed some of her most intimate secrets and she wasn't even sure who she was talking to.

"I'm Sandy. Pink helmet and six more freckles on my face than Cindy." But Sandy sounded almost absent-minded about that as she looked at Sara in dismay. "But Morgan is leaving!"

"Leaving for where?"

"He didn't say. I'm not sure he even knows. He just said he was leaving. He didn't want to see you and Brian together again."

Sara swallowed hard but tried not to panic. "When is he leaving?"

"Now! He was unhooking the electricity and sewer lines and putting things away in the motor home when I left the campground."

"Now?" Sara repeated. She looked at the long hill stretching ahead of her. She must be at least two miles from the campground. Morgan could be gone by the time she got there.

"You really love him?" Sandy demanded suddenly.

"I really love him."

Sandy checked Sara's wilted appearance, shoe decorated with sticky black stuff, the distance she had come and the distance she had yet to go. Apparently what she saw convinced her that Sara was sincere.

"Okay, you take my bicycle." She thrust the handlebars at Sara. "I'll walk back to the campground. Maybe you can get there before he leaves."

Sara didn't make polite objections to taking the bicycle and leaving Sandy afoot. She just grabbed it and started to get on.

"And take my helmet, too. You shouldn't be bicycling on the highway without one."

Sandy took off the helmet, shaking her head to loosen the blond hair clinging to her neck. Sara put the brilliant helmet on and fastened the strap under her chin.

"Thanks, Sandy." She paused for one question. "Did Morgan say he loved me?"

Sandy looked as if she wished she could answer that question yes, but she shook her head negatively. "Good luck," was all she said as she waved Sara off.

So maybe this frantic chase was all in vain. But Sara wasn't going to give up now.

It took her a few minutes to figure out the gears on the unfamiliar bicycle, and even after she did the hill was steep enough that the going wasn't easy. But then she had a chance to rest on the long, glorious coast down the other side of the hill. She calculated the distance remaining. One more hill, past a viewpoint at the top, then several dips and rises around a hill where the highway briefly turned inland. Down another long hill and then she'd be at the entrance to the campground.

She sent telepathic messages to Morgan: *Don't leave yet. I'm coming. Wait just a few more minutes. I'll be there. I love you!*

Her legs and back and lungs ached with the exertion for speed up the next hill. She hadn't even been on a bicycle in a couple of years except when Morgan had taken her to dinner. Her mouth was so dry that it felt like a pan burned empty on a hot stove.

Her telepathic messages grew less politely beseeching. *Morgan McKenzie, don't you dare leave! I'm working my buns off to get to you. Don't you dare run out on me now!*

Yet somehow, when she rounded the last highway curve, she wasn't surprised to see the big gray-and-burgundy motor home ready to pull onto the highway from the campground exit.

Sara waved wildly. He had to look her direction to check for oncoming traffic. Surely he'd see her.

It was all downhill from here. She shifted gears frantically to get all possible speed out of the bicycle.

Her voice followed her like a trailing siren as she raced down the hill. "Morg-a-a-a-n-n-n!"

## Chapter Eleven

The sleek motor home, like some giant silver-and-burgundy insect indifferent to the petty activities of mere humans, pulled onto the highway and started up the hill on the far side of the campground entrance. Sara reached the bottom of the hill with enough momentum to carry her a short distance up the other side. But even with her momentum the big motor home rapidly pulled away from her.

Valiantly she struggled after it, straining every muscle on the pedals. If she could get to the top of the hill maybe she could catch up with him going down the far side. There was a viewpoint just beyond the crest of the hill. Maybe he'd stop there for one last regretful or angry look back at Port Kesterson on the far side of the curved bay, and she could get there before he left. But as her legs tired and weakened, and the distance between the bicycle and the motor home widened, wilder ideas for catching up with or stopping Morgan flashed through her head.

Maybe she could flag down a police car and persuade some sympathetic officer, in the interests of true love, to go after him. No, a police officer wouldn't be interested in playing a siren-wielding Cupid; with her luck she'd more likely find herself detained by some suspicious officer to take a breath-analyzer test. Maybe she could tell the police that the driver of the motor home was some desperate criminal on the most-wanted list, that the motor home was hers and he'd just stolen it, or he was some dangerous international spy in disguise.

And just how happy would Morgan be to see her after he had to explain his way out of one of those wild accusations? And what kind of trouble would she be in for telling such tales?

Maybe she could call ahead and ask someone in Cougar Beach to flag him down. Or she might rush back to Port Kesterson's tiny airstrip and hire a helicopter to chase him down. She had momentary visions of herself landing on the roof of the motor home in flamboyant gangster-movie style.

But in the end, as she fell farther and farther behind the motor home and her tired legs gave out, the bicycle simply wobbled to a halt. In one last frustrated attempt to catch Morgan's attention, she stood in the bicycle lane and signaled with wild and fast jumping jacks, waving arms and legs as if she were trying to propel herself skyward.

*Look back, Morgan!* she commanded. *Look in your rearview mirror! Don't just run off and leave me!*

She knew people in passing cars were staring. What did they think? That this was some strange new mating dance of the pink-headed, sticky-footed, Oregon bicyclist? But she didn't care what they thought. She just jumped and waved more wildly. Wolf whistles floated back to her from a couple of cars.

Once she thought the motor home briefly slowed, but then, like some aloof aristocrat of the open road, it whizzed on.

In one final, futile gesture she picked up a handful of rocks beside the road and flung them after the departing vehicle. She may as well have been shooting arrows at the moon.

The motor home sailed majestically over the brow of the hill and disappeared.

Sara slumped by the side of the road, momentarily too tired even to climb on the bicycle and coast back down the hill. What now? She might be able to track Morgan down through his family or the literary agent Alana, but she had the empty feeling that it was too late. She'd had her chance when Morgan had come to Port Kesterson looking for her. And she'd blown it. This time, when he filed for divorce, he'd show up at the hearing.

She finally got on the bicycle again and started back down the hill. She felt as if this was where her whole life was headed: downhill. No more lover, husband and friend. No more sand-castle-building playmate.

Then the husky honk of a horn and roar of a big engine startled her. Sara half turned and saw the big motor home bearing down on her.

Morgan yelled something she couldn't hear and pointed to the wide turnout at the bottom of the hill. She saw total astonishment on his face just before the motor home roared by her. She didn't understand the surprise. Who else but love-crazy Sara McKenzie would be out here trying to chase down a motor home with a bicycle, making a complete spectacle of herself alongside the road?

He was standing by the vehicle waiting for her by the time she reached the turnout. He peered at her incredulously.

*"Sara?"*

Suddenly Sara realized what this was all about. Because she was wearing Sandy's unmistakable glow-pink helmet and riding Sandy's bicycle, he hadn't until the last minute realized that she wasn't who he thought she was.

"You thought I was Sandy. That's the only reason you came back," she accused as she stepped off the bicycle. She loosened the chin strap and yanked the helmet off her head.

"I came back because in my rearview mirror I saw what looked like some crazy person leaping up and down alongside the road. At first I thought maybe there had been an accident or something, but then the sun hit that helmet just right and...yes, I thought it was Sandy. I can't pull that big motor home off the road just anywhere so I had to go on up to the viewpoint to turn around."

"So now I suppose you're disappointed."

"So now I'm wondering why you're dashing around in Sandy's helmet. On Sandy's bike."

"Maybe I'm the notorious Bicycle Bandit." She set the helmet on the bicycle seat. "My specialty is waylaying unsuspecting blondes."

Morgan rolled his eyes and, because Sara apparently did not intend to explain details, dropped the subject of how she had acquired helmet and bicycle. "I want to know what this wild chase is all about. Did I leave a stray sock or something at your place? Or maybe you just wanted to run me down to announce your re-engagement to Brian and wave that overweight diamond ring under my nose again."

Sara blinked back tears of frustration and hurt and disappointment. She was tired and sweaty. Her legs ached and her back hurt. The sticky black goo on her shoe had somehow migrated to her leg. And this was not the open-arms welcome she had envisioned with such hope.

"Actually, you're right. You left a sock at my place." She snatched the white sock out of her jeans pocket and plastered it like a medal against his chest.

"You chased me down for this? And I thought *I* had problems with maturity," Morgan muttered.

"And I had this to give you, too." Sara yanked the envelope out of the other rear pocket of her jeans, ripped it open and slammed one of the two items it contained into his hand. "It was cluttering up my drawer."

Morgan ran a forefinger wonderingly around the inside of the golden circle. "My wedding ring. Where did you get it?"

"It was an accident. I didn't mean to take it. After I got down to my mother's I found it in that little jewelry box where I kept a few things. You must have put it there when you weren't wearing it after you hurt your hand on the chimney sweeping job." She blinked, remembering how she had cried when she'd found the ring. She was *not* going to cry now, she thought resolutely.

"Why did you save it?"

"It wasn't mine... to dispose of."

"And your ring?"

Sara had palmed the other ring. Reluctantly she opened her hand. The starburst of tiny diamonds on the wedding band glittered in the soft dusk gathering in this dip between hills. She stuffed the ring back into her jeans pocket.

"Why did you keep it?" he asked. "Why didn't you get rid of it along with the pair of crystal glasses from our anniversary? It was yours to 'dispose of.'"

Sara managed a shrug. "Foolish sentimentality, I suppose."

"Sara, do you know what I thought when I rushed to the lawyer and filed for that divorce?"

"I assume you were in a big hurry to divorce me."

"I thought when you got those legal-looking papers that you'd come rushing back to me. No doubt mad as hell, probably mad enough to cook them and make me eat them for dinner. But I thought you'd come back."

"And I thought you'd come to San Diego after me."

He shook his head regretfully. "We had so much growing up to do. We were playing foolish games, acting like irresponsible children." When she didn't say anything he added, "I didn't come just to get my stuff this morning. I came to see you. I thought we might talk things out. But I saw that you had already made a fast reconciliation with Brian. I suppose I should have offered congratulations. But I wasn't big-hearted enough to do it."

Sara briefly repeated the story of her pickup's demise and Brian's provision of transportation so she could look for a new truck. "Brian and I didn't have any reconciliation. He's going to Connecticut. I'm not."

"You're not re-engaged?"

"No."

"I see." Morgan twirled the wedding ring on his forefinger and eyed her reflectively. "So what are you going to do?"

"About what?"

"About me. You've run me down and roped me in like a cowboy after a stray calf. Now what? You must have had something you wanted to say. Surely just giving a sock and ring back to me wasn't important enough for you to...how shall I put it?...make a spectacle of yourself alongside the road."

"Making a spectacle of myself alongside a road seems to be a specialty of mine," Sara snapped, thinking of herself and a pickup-load of furniture strewn along Atherton Drive.

"Actually, there's nothing I like better than a good spectacle," Morgan said. The upper half of his face was still scowling, but the beginning of a smile quirked the corners of his mouth. "Remember the time we camped after dark in what we thought was a secluded little grove of trees and woke up to find we were on the edge of somebody's country mansion—"

"And the lady of the house was giving her local garden club a tour of the grounds, and there we were, frantically trying to get dressed in our double sleeping bag with all those nice little ladies standing around watching..."

Sara tried to scowl, too, but she couldn't. Her lower lip wobbled, and then suddenly they were both laughing. Morgan swept Sara up in his arms and whirled her around until her legs flew out.

"People are staring," Sara said breathlessly.

He didn't set her down. "Then let's really give them something to stare at."

Her feet were still off the ground as he kissed her. Her eyes closed and her arms clamped around his neck and she kissed him back. For long moments she wasn't conscious of anything but the two of them. The taste of his mouth, familiar and wonderful and exciting. The feel of his lips on hers, a breathtaking blend of soft and hard, tender and rough. The sound coming from somewhere deep in his throat, something between a sensuous growl and a rumble of approval. The feel of his arms holding her tight, and the length of his muscular body pressed hard against hers. The tingles that raced through her, tiny explosions of love and desire, raising havoc with her mind and senses.

Then a car went by honking so loudly that the sound penetrated even Sara's closed, breathless world. Someone yelled a risqué comment and several someones whistled raucously. Morgan ignored them.

"I'm sorry," he said huskily. "I'm sorry I didn't tell you everything at first. Sorry you got the impression I thought you were, as you kept putting it, a 'money-hungry gold digger.' Sorry I didn't march right over and yank you out of Brian's car this morning."

"And I'm sorry I didn't say 'yes!' right away when you came back. Sorry I didn't tell you I'd already decided to come back to you even before I knew you had sold the book and weren't a penniless drifter—"

He pushed her out to arm's length and looked down into her eyes. "Really?"

"Really. And I'm sorry I didn't jump out of Brian's car this morning and run to you."

"Are you sure, Sara? *Seeking Shawn* sold for more money than I ever thought possible, but life with a writer is never going to be quite as safe and secure as it would be with a banker. The book could be a complete flop, or I could be one of those one-book authors who never sells another word."

"I don't think the book is going to be a flop or that you're a one-book author—"

Morgan grinned with rakish confidence. "Neither do I. But I want you to be aware that it's *possible.*"

"But even if it did happen, nothing happens to *us*. I love *you*. For richer or poorer, remember?"

"We've been through the 'poorer' together, and I wouldn't have missed it for the world. But I'm not sorry that we now have the chance to try out the 'richer.' Alana has already seen the rough draft of my next book, and she tells me it's going to bring more than the last one." He kissed her on the nose. Then his voice went husky and rough with emotion. "I love you, Sara. I want to give you everything I never did before."

He kissed her again, pushing her up close to the motor home where they couldn't be seen from the highway. His hands roamed over her, and the kiss was more sensual, more lingering, more breathtaking. His tongue caressed her lips and penetrated deeper. One hand found her breast, and she moved her shoulder to return the caress against the pressure of his hand. He pressed her back against the motor home, trapping her between the muscular length of his body and the hard metal.

He kissed her throat, and she nibbled the softness of those irresistible earlobes.

A triple pound of fist on metal interrupted his soft murmur of loving words and startled them both.

"Well, of all the—" Sandy scowled at them and emphasized her indignant words with another slam of her fist. "I've been walking for *miles,* thinking every minute that you two would show up to rescue me. And now I find you just standing around making out like a couple of oversexed teenagers!"

Sara and Morgan separated bodies, but he kept an arm around her shoulders and she an arm around his waist.

"I started walking from town out to the campground. Sandy loaned me her bicycle so I could chase after you. I left her stranded on foot a couple miles back toward town," Sara explained to Morgan. "I guess I kind of forgot about you," she added guiltily to Sandy.

"I suppose you did have more important things to think about," Sandy agreed as she inspected Sara and Morgan. She picked up her pink helmet from the bicycle seat and suddenly smiled like a sly matchmaker. "I take it you two have ended the family feud and are getting back together?"

Sara and Morgan looked at each other. Sara expected him to say that the McKenzie family feud was indeed history, but he just tilted his head speculatively.

"I don't know if we can. Sara has been saying all along that we'll get back together when the ocean turns to champagne. So I guess we'll have to check that out first before we decide."

Sandy squinted in a bemused way as she looked at them, but she just slipped the helmet over her long blond hair and climbed on the bicycle. She eyed the sock still clinging to Morgan's shirt. "These are crazy people," she declared to no one in particular before she pedaled off.

Morgan opened the motor home door and motioned Sara inside. She assumed they were going back to her place, but Morgan drove the motor home across the highway to the campground entrance.

"What are we going to do here?" Sara asked, puzzled.

"I still have some time left on the week I paid for," Morgan explained. The gate attendant glanced at the "paid" sticker on the windshield of the motor home and waved them on through.

"But I thought—I mean— Why are we coming here?"

Morgan looked at her as if surprised. "Why, to check to see if the ocean has turned to champagne, of course."

Morgan parked the motor home at space thirty-seven. Sara had the churned-up feeling that the situation was nowhere near as settled as she had thought it was only a few moments earlier. What was going on here? Was Morgan just toying with her, paying her back for all she'd put him through? Playing another foolish game, after which he'd announce that since the ocean hadn't turned to champagne they weren't getting back together after all?

He went to a cupboard in the compact kitchen. "We'll need glasses, of course. We don't want to run this test by just sticking a finger in the sea and tasting it."

He selected two fragile, swirled-stem wineglasses set in a special rack to keep them from sliding around and breaking when the motor home was on the road. With a small flourish he handed one glass to Sara.

The sun had set, leaving the beach in a soft afterglow of rose-lilac clouds. Only a handful of people were still on the beach. Morgan didn't head directly for the water.

"Now where are we going?" Sara asked doubtfully as he grabbed her hand and headed up the beach. She felt a little foolish walking along with a wineglass dangling from her fingers.

"We have to choose just the right place for our taste test. I think those rocks up there will be just fine."

"Morgan, this is silly—"

He stopped short. "You don't think the ocean has turned to champagne? You don't think it's time for us to get back together?"

For whatever his reasons, he was apparently planning to go through with this farce. Sara just shrugged and didn't comment.

They reached the rocky area. At high tide it was covered with water, but at this point, with the tide about halfway in, waves were just beginning to break over the rocks and churn the tidepools. Morgan grabbed Sara's hand again and dragged her along as he peered among the rocks where pink-tan starfish clung with graceful tenacity and sea anemones looked like delicate, gray-green flowers blooming underwater.

Suddenly he stopped. "This is it. The just-right place for our taste test."

Apparently he intended to carry this through to the end. Sara steeled herself for some unhappy ending to what was beginning to feel like an elaborate bad joke.

Then he leaned forward. "And how about this—I believe the ocean really has turned to champagne! Look, it's all bottled and everything."

Sure enough, there, bobbing gently at the edge of a tide-pool, was a sealed bottle of something.

"But we'll have to taste it to be certain, of course." He handed his glass to Sara and fished the bottle out of the water. "Now I'll just open this—"

Like a magician working some private hocus-pocus, he turned his back on Sara. Suspicious of all these strange goings-on, she stepped around him to see what he was doing.

A fountain exploded between them as the cork popped. Bubbly liquid shot skyward and then rained back down on them. It landed in Sara's hair and dripped down her cheeks and nose. It did the same to Morgan, jeweling his hair and eyelashes. He grinned at her through the streams of bubbly liquid.

Sara reached out a finger and scooped up a stream trickling across his jaw. She tasted the drops.

"Champagne!" she decreed.

Morgan made a more intimate taste test. He ran his tongue across her lips, collecting the drops as they gathered there. The champagne made cold trickles across her face, but the drops felt fiery as he gathered them with his tongue.

He grinned at her and nodded. "It's a miracle!"

Sara leaned over to inspect the bottle. It was her old friend, that well-traveled bottle of Dom Perignon. Morgan saw that she recognized it.

"Semi-miracle?" he asked hopefully.

Sara smiled and held out the glasses for him to fill from the still-foaming bottle. Sloshing and bouncing in the surf was obviously not the ideal treatment to give a bottle of champagne just before opening. "Close enough," she declared.

They linked arms to drink the first sip, two people drenched with champagne and smiling with love.

And a moment later they were two people sprawling in the surf as a thigh-high wave rose to engulf them.

Morgan groaned as the wave receded with a swish and gurgle. Sara could almost swear it had a self-satisfied "gotcha" sound. He didn't try to stand up, just propped his head up with one hand. He eyed the bottle and glasses that had washed a half dozen feet up the beach. All were empty now.

"Morgan, you couldn't have planned all this—"

He groaned again. He sat up, legs crossed in front of him. "Of course not. You think I'd *plan* that we wind up soaked to the skin again?"

Sara sat up too, her knees touching his. "Actually, I think I'm beginning to like it. Maybe I'm part mermaid."

"I decided I couldn't take the bottle of champagne with me. I'd brought it to celebrate our getting back together, and I'd never be able to drink it without being reminded that we *hadn't* gotten back together. So I brought it down here and buried it in the sand between the rocks."

"And now the sea really is part champagne."

Morgan grinned. "The Mermaid Special—take one bottle of champagne. Mix well with one ocean."

"Add two people in love and stir gently."

He put his hands on her shoulders and leaned across the jumble of their crossed legs to kiss her. He looked serious and thoughtful, at least as serious and thoughtful as a man with mingled champagne and seawater dripping off him can look. Lapping waves of the rising tide swished around them, but neither of them noticed.

"I love you, Sara."

"I love you."

"We could go to a minister. Have a second wedding ceremony—"

"We could have our own ceremony right here, right now."

Sara dug her ring out of her jeans pocket and handed it to him. He handed the other larger, matching ring to her.

Gently he placed the smaller ring on her finger. "With this ring I thee wed," he said. He smiled. "Again."

She slid the other ring on the finger of his left hand. "With this ring I thee wed . . . still."

And as the rising tide swirled around them one or both of them echoed, "Forever."

# Epilogue

Sara watched the motor home recede down the road. She felt a certain pang as it disappeared around a bend.

Then Morgan's arm tightened around her shoulders. "No jumping jacks to try to stop it?" he asked with a smile. "No wild bicycle chase?"

Sara leaned her head against his shoulder. "I have everything I want right here." She touched his left hand clasping her shoulder and traced the solid golden circle around her finger. "Are you sorry to see it go?"

"We had our second honeymoon in it. So I suppose I have a certain sentimental attachment to it."

Then he turned her around to face the other direction. The house loomed before them, still smelling of new lumber and fresh paint. The windows shone red-gold with the reflection of the setting sun, and the steep roofline angled gracefully against the sky. A sea gull strutted along the railing of the upper deck that opened off the master bedroom. The freshly seeded lawn was just coming up, the sprigs of grass bright green against the dark earth. The surf swished against the gentle slope of sand below them, the sound punctuated by deeper booms where it churned around the ragged rocks farther down the beach. Her "back-to-the-wedding" present, the very house he'd once dragged her out here to see.

"We could go in and start unpacking and putting things away," Sara said. The cat, which she no longer thought of as stray, wound around their legs as if weaving them together.

"We could . . . but let's go down to the beach and build a sand castle instead."

Sara looked at him with love in her heart and laughter in her eyes. Morgan had matured. He'd put down roots and traded the motor home as part payment on the house. His second book had sold, and movie offers were already coming in on the first one. In about seven months he'd be a father, a fact that filled him with so much pride and happiness that he was already proclaiming it to the world. But he'd always be her playmate as well.

She grabbed his hand and raced for the beach.

\*   \*   \*   \*   \*

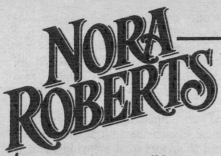

# NORA ROBERTS

Love has a language all its own, and for centuries, flowers have symbolized love's finest expression. Discover the language of flowers—and love—in this romantic collection of 48 favorite books by bestselling author Nora Roberts.

Starting in February, two titles will be available each month at your favorite retail outlet.

In March, look for:

*Irish Rose*, **Volume #3**
*Storm Warning*, **Volume #4**

In April, look for:

*First Impressions*, **Volume #5**
*Reflections*, **Volume #6**

Collect all 48 titles and become fluent in

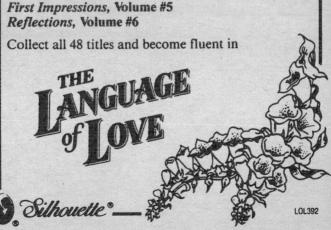

# THE LANGUAGE of LOVE

# WORD SEARCH CONTEST

You can win a year's supply of Silhouette romances ABSOLUTELY FREE! All you have to do is complete the word puzzle below and send it to us so we receive it by April 30, 1992. The first 10 properly completed entries chosen by random draw will win a year's supply of Silhouette romances (four books every month, two from the Special Edition® and two from the Intimate Moments® series—worth over $160.00). What could be easier?

```
K  L  E  B  R  O  K  N  E  E  L  H  T  A  K  M  C  E
V  A  R  P  V  A  E  D  F  G  E  L  S  F  O  R  M  G
R  N  O  O  S  I  R  E  M  L  A  P  A  N  A  I  D  S
O  O  X  M  G·R  V  F  S  E  O  N  S  E  L  T  I  T
M  C  J  P  R  Y  E  E  D  O  V  B  Y  I  J  A  O  N
A  E  B  A  D  T  G  V  W  I  G  O  E  C  S  R  O  E
N  D  T  Q  M  A  N  P  O  L  F  R  L  E  T  A  F  M
C  R  G  T  P  N  I  V  L  C  I  U  R  A  R  I  N  O
E  A  E  R  E  T  N  R  U  C  Q  I  U  W  E  N  Y  M
K  W  Z  E  G  U  W  A  H  L  S  H  H  B  V  W  E
F  O  L  N  T  E  O  A  K  E  L  P  O  R  O  I  L  T
Z  H  G  I  D  U  R  H  D  O  A  N  E  P  R  L  V  A
B  A  O  P  A  D  B  C  L  O  G  B  H  O  A  L  I  M
E  D  N  S  S  V  E  T  Y  I  M  A  T  X  R  E  D  I
A  N  F  A  E  Z  I  W  X  A  S  L  E  E  O  C  A  T
Y  I  U  S  N  A  X  E  T  L  L  A  T  G  N  O  L  N
S  L  E  K  D  F  I  U  R  M  J  E  A  N  L  H  O  I
W  N  O  I  T  I  D  E  L  A  I  C  E  P  S  E  D  F
```

| | | |
|---|---|---|
| LOVE | TITLES | EMILIE RICHARDS |
| NORA ROBERTS | ANN MAJOR | DESIRE |
| COVERS | THE O'HURLEYS | PAGES |
| SILHOUETTE | RITA RAINVILLE | LONG TALL TEXANS |
| DIXIE BROWNING | INTIMATE MOMENTS | DIANA PALMER |
| ROMANCE | SPINE | KATHLEEN KORBEL |
| LINDA HOWARD | SPECIAL EDITION | |

*Please turn over for entry details*

# HOW TO ENTER

All the words listed are hidden in the word puzzle grid. You can find them by reading the letters forward, backward, up and down, or diagonally. When you find a word, circle it or put a line through it. Don't forget to fill in your name and address in the space provided, put this page in an envelope, and mail it today to:

Silhouette Word Puzzle Contest
Silhouette Reader Service™
P.O. Box 9071
Buffalo, NY 14269-9071

NEXT MONTH:
LOOK FOR YOUR CHANCE
TO WIN A COLLECTOR'S
EDITION, AM/FM
OLD-TIME RADIO!!!!

NAME _____

ADDRESS _____

_____

CITY _____ STATE _____ ZIP CODE _____

## Rules

1. All eligible contest entries must be recieved by April 30, 1992.
2. Ten (10) winners will be selected from properly completed entries in a random drawing from all entries on or about July 1, 1992. Odds of winning are dependent upon the number of entries received. Winners will be notified by mail. Decisions of the judges are final. Winners consent to the use of their name, photograph or likeness for advertising and publicity in conjunction with this and similar promotions without additional compensation.
3. Winners will receive four (4) Silhouette romance novels (two (2) from the Special Edition® and two (2) from the Intimate Moments® series) per month for one (1) year, with a total retail value of $162.72.
4. Open to all residents of the U.S., 18 years or older, except employees and families of Torstar Corporation, its affiliates and subsidiaries.

S2MAR2

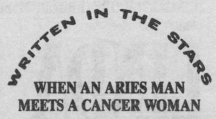

From the popular author of the bestselling title
DUNCAN'S BRIDE (Intimate Moments #349)
comes the

# LINDA HOWARD
## COLLECTION

Two exquisite collector's editions that contain four of
Linda Howard's early passionate love stories. To add
these special volumes to your own library, be sure
to look for:

**VOLUME ONE:**  *Midnight Rainbow*
*Diamond Bay*
(Available in March)

**VOLUME TWO:**  *Heartbreaker*
*White Lies*
(Available in April)

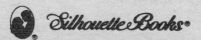

SLH92